Circle of Fire

Circle of Fire

S.M. Hall

F

FRANCES LINCOLN
CHILDREN'S BOOKS

First published in Great Britain and in the USA in 2011 by
Frances Lincoln Children's Books, 4 Torriano Mews,
Torriano Avenue, London NW5 2RZ
www.franceslincoln.com

A catalogue record for this book is available from the British Library.

ISBN 978-1-84780-121-0

Set in Palatino

Printed in Croydon, Surrey, UK by CPI Bookmarque Ltd.
in December 2010.

1 3 5 7 9 8 6 4 2

For Hannah, who is as brave and feisty as Maya,
and for the new generation, Riber, Charlie and Sebbie.
My thanks to Pam Royds, Caroline Knox,
Mark Roberts and to Emily Sharratt
and Maurice Lyon at Frances Lincoln - S.M.H.

Chapter One

Maya opened her eyes to a room full of shadows. A drumming sound filled her head. When she tried to sit up, a long, thin strand of wire wrapped around her neck. Panic gripped her until she realised it was her iPod – she'd gone to sleep with music plugged into her ears.

Pulling out the earphones, she switched off the music and gazed round the room. Moonlight was seeping in through the open window, silver light glinted on the glass, gauzy curtains flapped in the breeze.

She swung her legs out of bed and sprang to her feet. What an idiot! She'd forgotten to close the window. Her eyes swept the room, darting over every blurry surface, her ears strained for any sound.

Was somebody hiding? Was someone in the room watching her? She waited, hardly daring to breathe. Everything was quiet. No strange sounds or creaks.

Telling herself there was nothing to worry about, she padded over to the window and looked out. A silver moon hung like a giant coin over the dark hills. In the garden below, familiar shapes were fuzzy and blurred; the lawn rippled with swirling patterns. Then she heard it – the crunch of gravel underfoot. She leaned out of the window and saw a dense black shape sliding towards the corner of the house.

The neon alarm clock showed it was almost midnight. She wasn't sure whether the shape had been human or animal, moonlight could play tricks. Was there a prowler? For a few moments she stood listening, but there were no more sinister sounds, just the breeze stirring the trees.

Quietly she closed the window, fastened the security latch, then she undressed, put on her pyjamas and slipped out of her room into the bathroom. On the way back she saw light coming from under her mum's door.

She knocked tentatively and pushed open the door. Her mum, Pamela, was sitting at her desk working on a laptop.

'What's the matter, darling? Can't you sleep?'

Maya stepped into the room. 'Something woke me. You didn't hear anything, did you?'

'No.'

Pam hadn't taken her eyes off the screen; her fingers were still tapping at the keyboard.

Maya hesitated, wondering whether to say more. Her mum seemed absorbed in her work. 'OK. I'll leave you to it, then.'

'Right,' Pam replied tersely, but just as Maya was closing the door, she relented. 'Sorry, Maya. I'm trying to get this report finished. What did you hear?'

'Oh, nothing really. I dropped off to sleep and left my window open, the curtains were blowing about.'

The typing stopped. Pam stood up. 'The alarm's on. If anybody's out there, the sensors will pick it up. Did you close the window?'

Maya nodded. 'Yeah. I'm sure everything's fine now.'

Pam came over and put her arms round Maya's waist. 'I'll contact Security; they'll be out there all night. You probably heard one of their men checking the back of the house.'

'Mmm, I s'pose that's who it was.'

While Pam picked up her radio and spoke to

Security, Maya rested her chin on top of her mum's head and Pam hugged her close, massaging her back and neck.

'Everything's OK,' she said, clicking the radio off. 'I'm sorry you were frightened. This will all be over soon, I promise.'

'I wasn't frightened. I'm just tired of hiding. Sometimes I wish they'd show themselves – make some attempt to get me.'

'No,' Pam said sharply. 'That's exactly why we're here. I don't want you in danger.'

'But I want to know who they are. I want to see them busted – clapped in jail.'

'I'm working on it,' Pam said.

At that moment, the mobile phone lying on her desk buzzed. 'Oh, not at this hour,' she moaned. Picking it up, she checked the screen. 'It's Simon.'

Maya was all ears. Simon was her mum's second in command, so she listened carefully, hoping to pick up some secret, and at the same time seized the opportunity to sit at her mum's desk and scan the computer screen.

The phone conversation yielded nothing, all Pam did was listen. But the text on the screen was intriguing.

The chain of command operates on a p
system. In this way each cell is separate but also part
of an international network. The organisation known as the
Brotherhood thus poses a threat of. . .

'Hey, that's classified information.' Pam swivelled Maya away from the computer.

'Sorry, can't help it. Radar switched on at all times. Who taught me that?'

Pam gave Maya a rueful smile and reached for her hand, pulling her out of the chair. 'You need to get some sleep.'

I'm not the only one, Maya thought, noting the dark circles under her mum's eyes. 'Are you going to be up all night?' she asked.

Pam sighed. 'This investigation is growing by the minute.'

'Tell me.'

'I can't.'

'It's not just about the threat to kidnap me any more, is it?'

'No. But, look, it's way too late to discuss it and anyway all information is—'

There had been little else to occupy Maya's mind over the past few days – now she cut sharply across her mum's words.

'A group of would-be terrorists threatened to kidnap me because they wanted to frighten you off, to stop your investigation. They're plotting something – something big.'

Pam raised her eyebrows and nodded. 'I'm impressed.'

Maya's dark eyes were intense, her expression eager. 'Until you've managed to smash their organisation and trap the leaders, I've got to stay here under guard.'

'I'm afraid so,' Pam said. 'This is turning into the biggest operation the Security Service has ever seen. Intelligence units nationwide – MI5, MI6 – overseas outfits. It's a major threat, a huge responsibility.'

Maya saw her mum's shoulders tense, her eyes flash with the steely determination she was renowned for. She put out her hand and touched Maya's cheek. 'But, I've almost cracked it, we're nearly ready to move.'

'Mum, you will be careful, won't you?'

'I'm always careful.'

Maya looked away, staring towards the darkened window. 'They're Muslims, aren't they? Islamic terrorists?'

'Yes.'

'Maniacs wanting to blow up the whole world.'

'Maya. . . ' Her mother didn't finish, instead, she gave Maya a troubled look.

'I know,' Maya said. 'Not all Muslims are extremists.'

Pam pursed her lips and blew a stream of air up over her face. Her eyes sought Maya's and she held her gaze.

'You of all people should know that,' Pam said quietly.

Maya was silent; half-forgotten sounds and pictures bloomed in her head. She blinked, surprised by the sudden vivid kaleidoscope – bursting shells, falling debris, a sharp smell of burning.

'It's all right to remember,' her mother said.

Maya looked away.

There had been no secrets, she had been told that her family had been murdered in Kosovo – picked out by Serbs because they were Muslim. If Pam hadn't rescued Maya she would have died too. Most people in her village had been wiped out.

'There are extremists on all sides. They're the people I deal with,' Pam said.

'I hate religion,' Maya muttered. 'It sends people mad.'

Pam grimaced. 'I haven't done a very good job, have I?'

'Why should I believe in anything? If my family hadn't, they'd still be alive.'

'Your people were Muslim.'

'I don't feel any connection, sorry.' Maya's face hardened as she turned away.

Pam changed the subject. 'You still up for that run in the morning?'

'Yeah. Not much else to do round here.'

'It'll be an early start. Seven all right?'

'I suppose so.'

As her mum reached for a file at the back of the desk a photo fluttered to the floor. Maya picked it up. Taken on her fifteenth birthday, just a few weeks ago, it showed her and Pam in khaki combat suits, arms round each other, grinning at the camera. They'd just completed a challenging assault course.

'I loved that day,' Maya said. 'Best birthday ever.'

Pam smiled. 'You aced me on the shooting, you were a natural.'

'And I did a good time on the racing circuit,' Maya said.

Pam had organised the day at the Police Training

Academy as a birthday treat – a rare day spent together – and they'd had so much fun. It had fuelled Maya's ambition – it was exciting, exacting, dangerous. She wanted to follow in her mum's footsteps. She just wished she could start the training right away, instead of having to spend five more years at school and university.

'Couldn't I do something to help?' she asked.

Pam waved the file. 'I just need one last piece of data. Then, when I've turned in my report, we act, quickly, swiftly – dawn raids, house arrests. If we succeed, the world will be a safer place. And you can go back to school and your friends.'

Maya grinned. 'Go get 'em, Mum.'

Pam put the file on the desk, opened it and switched back to business mode. She sat down in front of the computer her fingers hovering over the keyboard. 'OK. So, now I need to finish this report.'

Maya started to back out of the room, but she couldn't resist one last question. 'What did Simon want?'

Her mum's hands dropped to her lap; she sat still for a moment, head bowed then she swivelled round and looked at Maya. 'He gave me some data from a surveillance team.' Her eyes darted away, then back again. She ran her tongue across the top of her teeth. 'Look, I'm going to trust you with something.'

Maya took a step forward, her eyes locked with Pam's. 'What?'

'There are things in this report that even Simon doesn't know. This investigation is so sensitive – it's a political time bomb. I'm the only person who has access to all the files. Tomorrow I'm meeting an informant in Leeds. He's someone I trust but should anything go wrong, I want you remember something.'

'What?'

'A password.'

'What, what is it?'

'Firecracker.'

The word snapped and sizzled as if Pam had spat it into a flame. Maya felt a tingle of excitement fizz in her stomach. She could taste the word on her tongue, she wouldn't forget it – *Firecracker*.

Chapter Two

When Maya's alarm went off next morning, she wished she hadn't been so quick to agree to an early start. As she tied her running shoes she felt wobbly and light-headed – a night of disturbed sleep had taken its toll.

In the kitchen, Helen, Maya's grandmother, had just finished feeding the cluster of cats that hung around the cottage, and was washing out the empty cans. 'Did you sleep all right, dear?' she asked.

'Not really,' Maya said.

'No. You look tired,' Helen said, eyeing her closely. 'What you need is some fun.'

'Chance would be a fine thing,' Maya answered.

'Well, we'll have to see what we can do,' Helen said, stacking the cans on the draining board and then wiping her hands. 'There's a barn dance down at the village hall next week.'

Maya raised her eyebrows. 'Wow! Cool!'

'No need to be sarcastic. A quick do-si-do would do you the world of good,' Helen said, her eyes crinkling with laughter. 'Here,' she added, reaching into the fridge and pulling out a carton of juice. 'If you're off for a run, you need energy.'

'Mum's coming too,' Maya said, stretching out her legs. 'We're doing the loop, through the woods, down the lane to the ford and back up the hill.'

'It makes me dizzy just thinking about it.' Helen said. She poured some juice into a glass. 'Drink this before you go.'

Maya took the glass and sipped the ice-cold juice.

'Do the bodyguard people know you're going out?'

'Yep, Mum told them. Don't worry, they'll be tracking us all the way.'

'And a good thing too.'

'I know,' Maya agreed. 'I'm glad they're around, but sometimes I'd just like to . . . feel free.' Her eyes took on a faraway look. 'I'm missing loads at school, and then summer holidays'll be starting soon.

12

All my friends will be doing stuff together.'

'Hopefully it won't be for much longer,' Gran said, with a sympathetic smile. 'Then you can get back to London. Although I must say, I like having you here.'

'Love you too,' Maya said, giving Helen a quick kiss. 'Tell Mum I'm waiting outside.'

The sun was already bright, the dewy lawn sparkling like a giant lake, the flower beds flaming with colour – so different from the previous night when Maya had peered down onto a shadowy garden of fuzzy grey shapes. She stood with her hands on her hips, scanning the paths and soft soil beds, looking for a trace of the dark shifting shadow that had disturbed her sleep. There was nothing. Somebody or something had crunched the gravel at midnight but had left no trace, no footprints.

Her eyes lifted to the place where the hills humped and hollowed, where the dark woods lay. She stared until her eyes watered, wondering if anyone was out there – not the bodyguards, as Helen called them, but the terrorists who had threatened to take her hostage.

Behind her, the door opened and Pam appeared, humming a tune. She looked so bright-eyed and cheerful that Maya's dark thoughts quickly disappeared – early morning was the best time for running.

Before setting off, they did a few stretches together and Maya realised how much she'd grown, and how tiny Pam was in comparison. They were almost opposites, Pam's figure trim and compact in running gear, her freckled skin pale against a navy vest, her fine blonde hair held back with a white band. Beside her, Maya was like a rangy racehorse; long brown legs and arms, inky-black hair cascading down her back and dark brown, velvety eyes. It's no wonder people did a double take when Pamela introduced Maya as her daughter. It probably didn't take them long to work out that Maya was adopted.

Screwing her hair into a ponytail, Maya waited while Pam dashed into the kitchen for a quick drink of water. When she came out she was talking into her radio, informing the duty agents about their intended movements.

'OK. We're sorted,' she said.

Together they set off across the back lawn, slipped through a gap in the hedge and out into the open meadow. Here they took the path through the long grass down towards the woods. Under the trees Maya saw two figures waiting and watching for them. By the time they entered the cool darkness of the trees, the figures had disappeared.

Striding out together, their footsteps pounded hard mud, sunlight filtered through the branches, dappling their arms. When the path narrowed, Maya sucked in more air and increased her speed, running ahead. She sniffed the rich, earthy smell of the pine trees, enjoying the easy rhythm of her stride and the feeling of strength in her body. She ducked under a low branch, skirted round a fallen log and ran on through the tunnel of trees until she reached the other side of the wood. At the stile she paused and looked back. For a moment she thought Pam had stopped, but then she came out of the thicket and ran panting towards her.

When she was alongside Maya, Pam stood still and leaned forward with her hands on her hips, breathing heavily. 'Whoa, you set a cracking pace. How come you've improved so much?'

Maya beamed a crooked smile. 'The running machine at school. I wasn't allowed out at lunchtime, remember?'

'OK. No need to rub it in,' Pam said, straightening up and shaking out the muscles in her legs.

Behind her mother's shoulder Maya saw a movement in the bushes and caught a glimpse of a tall man with grey hair. The security agents were trying to keep pace with them. She smiled to herself – she'd give them a good workout.

'Let's go,' she said, and putting her hand on the stile, she vaulted it neatly and set off.

Rambling gorse bushes and spiky nettles narrowed the path to the lane, making it slow going for a few yards, but then there was open land and Maya flew across it to reach the kissing gate. She squeezed through and was out onto the open road, where she relaxed into an easy stride, allowing Pam to catch up.

The sun was full on their faces as they jogged side by side down the lane. There were swathes of buttercups and red campions in the hedges, the bushes were bright with birdsong and Maya felt her spirits lift. It was lovely to be out so early when they had the lanes to themselves. No chattering ramblers, no traffic, and better still, the security agents were keeping their distance, giving them some space.

The sleek silver Mercedes parked in a gateway was a surprise, hidden from view until they were almost in front of it.

Pam, breathing hard to keep up, didn't notice the driver leaning back against the field gate, a mobile to his ear, but Maya saw him and thought it strange. He didn't look the country type in his sleek, shiny suit and sunglasses. A quick snapshot registered – thick dark hair, brown skin, short grey beard, medium height, a bit overweight. What was he doing there? The glare of his eyes was on her back as she ran down the lane, and she had to admit to herself then that she was glad the security agents were shadowing them.

At the ford Pam ran ahead, skittering down the bank, making a big deal of waving her arms about, balancing on stepping stones with exaggerated clowning movements.

'You'll fall,' Maya shouted and, sure enough, one of Pam's trainers squelched into the mud.

'Serves you right,' Maya mocked.

Pam tried to catch her to push her in, but Maya was too fast.

'This was supposed to be a serious training run,' Maya protested.

Pam laughed. 'Remember how you used to love me driving the car through this ford?' she asked, wiping her muddy trainer on the grassy bank.

'Yeah,' Maya agreed. 'When I was five and it was full of water. We'd get stuck in the mud now.'

'That's global warming for you,' Pam said, as they clambered up the bank.

'Race you back home,' Maya challenged, running ahead.

The road back to the cottage was the most taxing part of the course – a long uphill climb. Maya ran with long even strides, her arms pumping.

Approaching a sharp bend, she slowed slightly, wiping sweat from her forehead, then looked up at a sudden squeal of brakes. Rushing towards her was a silver car. It had taken the bend too fast and was on the wrong side of the road. Maya yelled out to Pam, at the same time flinging herself towards the hedge. Thorns scraped her arms, flying grit stung her eyes.

The car just missed them. When she turned round, Pam was picking herself up off the tarmac.

'Stupid idiot,' Pam yelled.

Maya wiped her eyes and rubbed at her arms where the thorns had scratched.

'Good job we're OK,' Maya said. 'No thanks to him.'

The silver car had stopped a little way ahead. It was the Mercedes she'd spotted earlier. Pam started to stride towards it, eager to tell the driver just what she thought of him, but she didn't get the chance. Tyres skidding, the car roared off up the lane.

While Pam threw a few curses after it, Maya heard the sound of another car engine behind them. A big black vehicle came cruising up the lane towards them. It stopped when it was just a few metres away – a jeep with tinted windows, more army vehicle than car, it took up most of the road and sat with its engine purring.

Maya only had time to exchange an inquiring glance with her mum before the car doors swung open. Her eyes goggled as hooded men sprang out and stormed towards them waving guns.

'Get down! Down!' they screamed.

Before Maya could react, two black hoods flew towards her. One of them grabbed her head, forcing it backwards, fingers snaked round her neck, an arm circled her shoulders, her wrists were wrenched painfully up her back. She twisted and kicked, frothing with pain.

'Mum!' she yelled, but immediately a hand clamped her mouth.

She tried to bite the fleshy palm, squirmed sideways, stabbing out with her elbows, kicking at the men's legs, but it was no use, there were two of them holding her.

This was it. This was what she'd dreaded. They'd come to kidnap her. Where were the security agents? Her body went limp as she watched three hooded men surrounding Pam, targeting guns at her head and body. Pam had her hands partly raised and was talking fast, saying something in sharp, urgent tones. Maya couldn't hear what it was but one of the men nodded, then raised his hand and made a forward motion. Two of the men seized Pam's arms and started dragging her towards the jeep.

Don't take her, don't take her! Maya wanted to shout, but her captor's hand was jammed so hard over her mouth and nose that she could hardly breathe. Her legs were shaking violently, her bones rattling with shock, then her body jerked as a crack of gunfire shattered the air. One of the men holding Pam wheeled backwards and fell.

Maya gave a strangled scream, fighting to free herself, but the men holding her were too strong;

even when they began shooting towards the hedge their grip on her didn't relax. She was terrified that she would be hit as bullets whistled back and forth.

The Security Agents hiding behind the hedge yelled to her, 'Keep down! Down!' But Maya couldn't dodge down, she was a prisoner, directly in the firing line. Bullets zinged past her, hitting the jeep; one of her captors yelled and let go, falling to the ground. She tried to shake herself free as a flash of fire screamed over her head towards the hedge.

'Let's go! Let's go!' one of the assailants shouted.

Then all hell was let loose. Gunfire blazed back and forth. Maya was shoved to the ground, falling onto the gritty road. Gravel burned her hands and cheek, she tasted dirt.

Above the sound of gunshots she heard her mum screaming for her to run. But she couldn't run, she couldn't move or make a sound, she was frozen with fear. There was another thunderclap of fire towards the hedge, then shiny black boots crunched past her head, running towards the jeep. Doors banged shut, an engine revved and the vehicle skidded and slewed off up the road, disappearing from sight.

Silence gathered round her. Tears burned in her eyes, a blackbird sang in a nearby bush, soft wind rustled the leaves. Slowly, uncertainly, Maya pulled herself up and lurched to her feet.

'Are you all right?' A man she recognised as one of the security team came limping towards her, his sleeve covered in blood, a radio dangling from his hand.

'Yes,' Maya said. 'I'm OK.'

'They got Danny,' he told her, pointing to the hedge.

Maya looked and saw a pair of trainers sticking out of the long grass. She gasped. 'We have to help him.'

Stumbling up the bank she went closer, bending down she parted the leafy branches. He was wearing jeans, just ordinary denim jeans, but his shirt, a pale blue cotton shirt, was splashed with dark blood, and there was a bloody mess where the top of his head should have been. There was nothing anybody could do. His blood was flowing into the earth soaking the ground beneath the bright buttercups. It was Danny, a young agent who had played cheesy music, singing along to it as he'd driven her to school. His voice blared into her head; she remembered him telling her about his young son, she'd laughed at his bad jokes. Now he was dead, his blue eyes staring up at the sky.

'Bloody radio's smashed . . . no signal on my mobile phone,' the wounded agent rasped, slumping down onto the bank beside her. He winced as he tried to move his arm, pain scarred his face. 'We saw the car . . . the Merc.' His words tumbled out in jagged pieces. 'Danny ran a check . . . if we hadn't stopped to do that . . . we'd have been here in time. Christ! What a mess.'

Maya looked at him with glazed eyes. She felt nothing. What had just happened was unbelievable – a nightmare, a horror film. An agent was dead and her mum gone – driven away to God knew where.

Chapter Three

Maya's brain was in shock, her thoughts slippery as worms. Precious seconds ticked away while the wounded agent dripped blood and yelled into his defunct radio. He was in a bad state, a bullet had fractured his arm and his leg was bleeding heavily. She had to get help.

Lurching forward, she scanned the road, hoping desperately to see a vehicle she could flag down, but nothing appeared, no truck or car, not even a tractor.

Think, Maya, think. Focus, focus.

With a trembling hand she pinched her bloody nose, threw back her head. Blood trickled into her throat, sharp, metallic.

Get help! Run, you idiot, run. Run, go for help, go, go!

'You stay here,' she shouted to the wounded agent. 'I'll run to the cottage.'

Her trembling legs were slow to respond, she stumbled up the lane and clumsily climbed the stile onto the footpath. Then adrenalin kicked in. Desperation banished pain from her limbs.

Through the wood her feet grew wings, pounding the hard earth. Dark shadows haunted the bushes, twigs cracked like gunfire. Her breath was hot in her throat, leaves glinted like watching eyes. She ran faster than she'd ever run, racing home.

The path crumbled, pitching her down to a stream, feet sliding, fingers clawing. She scrabbled to find a foothold, then leapt, flying over silver water. Safe on the other side, she clambered uphill.

Run, Maya, run.

The path opened out into a meadow. Sun dazzled her eyes, grass tickled her calves. She headed for a dark band of bushes, thick as a secret. Thrusting the branches aside she uncovered a hidden stile, then, with a last pulse of energy, she sprang upwards, bursting from the thicket onto the edge of the cottage lawn.

She was shouting as she hurled herself through the back door into the kitchen. 'Gran!'

Helen's eyes goggled at the sight of her crazed granddaughter; flowers fell from her hands, a vase tilted, spilling water.

'It's Mum!' Maya shrieked. She grabbed at the kitchen table, her hands bloody and torn. 'They got Mum.' Her arms gave way. Pain and desperation surged through her as she collapsed onto a chair.

Gran's arms were round her, squeezing Maya's bruised shoulders. She was breathing hard. 'Who? Who's got her?'

'Men in a black jeep, five of them. They had guns. They didn't take me, they took Mum.'

'Where? When?'

'In Vicar's Lane, that bad bend, past the ford. We've got to get help. Danny was killed, the other security man's injured.'

Helen went white. 'Oh, my God,' she gasped. 'What can I do? What can we do? OK, right. . . You sit there. I . . . I'll call an ambulance and the police.'

Maya clutched her bloody knees while Helen talked to the emergency services. She heaved in great gasps. She couldn't think straight, her head was swirling, but she was conscious of something nagging at her, something she had to do. Simon.

She had to contact Simon. There was a special number for Pam's department. What was it? She'd phoned it loads of times.

Think, think. Yes, she remembered.

Running out into the hall she picked up the house phone and dialled. It felt like an eternity passed before she was connected; the phone buzzing as she held the receiver jammed to her ear. Her insides were juddering, deep shock chilled her bones. Her mind probed and prodded, questions burnt in her brain. Where was her mum? Where had the armed men taken her? What would they do to her?

Then there was a man's voice.

'Hello. This is Simon Maundsley.'

'I'm Maya, Maya Brown.' Her words started to tumble out in a shrill, high-pitched voice. He told her to slow down.

'It's Mum, she's been taken hostage. Please help, please!'

A loud intake of breath signalled his shock, but his manner was immediately brusque and businesslike. At that moment it was exactly what was needed.

Maya did her best to answer his questions, forcing her mind to track back over every painful detail. When she got to the final part – doors slamming, the jeep driving off, Danny dead – the phone shook in her hand, violent tremors wracked her body, her voice broke into jagged pieces.

'OK, that's enough,' Simon said. 'You get yourself sorted. I'm going to need your help. I'll mobilise the department. Don't worry, we'll do everything we can.'

Maya nodded vacantly while Simon told her he was on his way and that he would alert various agencies, but she was only half-listening; in her head a DVD was on permanent playback – skidding tyres, doors slamming, guns waving – fear, panic, pain. She remembered the hard grip of hands restraining her; she couldn't move, could hardly breathe. Pam was arguing with them. Then she saw the empty staring eyes of Danny, the young agent. She pressed her hands over her face, but the film didn't stop.

Mum, Mum where are you?

It didn't seem real. How could it? Half an hour ago Pam had been grabbing a quick drink of water in the kitchen before they set off on their run. At the stile she'd joked, saying Maya's new running shoes were magic, at the ford she'd been clowning around, her cheeks pink, her blonde hair damp with sweat.

Maya's eyes misted with tears. She was only

vaguely aware of Helen putting a drink of tea in front of her, then holding it to her lips. 'Drink this, you need it.'

Maya gave her a cracked smile and managed to say, 'Thank you.'

Helen was making a brave effort; she held Maya's hand, fetched a coat and put it round her shoulders.

'Here, you'll catch a chill,' she said, tucking the coat around her. Stroking Maya's hair, she cuddled her tight. 'It'll be all right, it'll be all right,' she murmured.

Maya couldn't respond. When Helen put a bowl of warm water on the table and bathed her bloody hands and knees, tenderly swabbing grit from the wounds, Maya didn't care how much it hurt – the pain was almost welcome. She wished she could have done something to help her mum, wished she could have helped the agents. If only she'd taken her mobile, she could have phoned the local cops right away and they might have stopped the jeep. It was all wrong, everything was hopeless – her Mum would be miles away by now.

She imagined Pam stuffed into the back seat of the jeep, wedged in between the armed men.

She'd be going crazy. She wasn't used to feeling helpless, she was always strong and positive, always in command. Closing her eyes Maya sent her a message.

Don't give them any trouble, Mum. Do as they say. I'm sorry I was useless. I promise I'll help find you.

While Helen prised some grit from the deepest cut on her hand, Maya told her, 'It was me they threatened. They should have taken me.'

'Don't blame yourself, my love,' Helen said. 'In the end it was your mum they wanted. Pam got too close to them, she knew too much.'

Maya knew her words were true. 'But how would the kidnappers know?' she demanded. 'How would they know what she'd discovered, unless. . .' She winced at the sting of antiseptic on her cuts. 'Unless some slimy, double-crossing bastard betrayed her.'

Helen finished winding a bandage round Maya's wrist and gently but firmly tied the ends. 'I suppose both sides are watching each other,' she said quietly. 'But your mum's got the best team. She's been in worse situations than this. They'll rescue her.'

Maya wished she could feel so sure; an image

of a hooded man flashed into her head – those men were murderers, she'd seen the hate in their eyes.

Gran hoisted herself to her feet and pulled Maya close, stroking her face. 'Are you going to be all right?'

'Yep. I've got to be.'

'That's my girl,' Helen said, kissing the top of Maya's head. 'We'll get through this – all three of us.'

'Yeah,' Maya said. 'We will but, oh, Gran, poor Danny – his wife, his son. It's horrible.' Her jaw trembled as she spoke, her words faltered and her chest heaved big, dry, gulping sobs.

Helen clutched her tightly, rubbing at her back and shoulders. Then she cupped Maya's chin, tilted her head back and looked her full in the face. 'It wasn't your fault – don't go thinking that – nor your mother's. What happened is dreadful, but the terrorists are to blame. They hold life cheap.' She kissed Maya's forehead. 'Oh, my darling, you shouldn't be mixed up in all this.'

Maya swallowed hard. 'It's all right, Gran. I'm OK.'

Helen gave her a small, forced smile. 'Good girl.' Her eyes were tearful as she turned away and bent to pick up the basin of bloody water.

Maya stared at the flowers Helen had been arranging. Something else was niggling at her, but her mind was so muddled. . .

Think, think!

She rubbed at her cheek where gravel had grazed it, and suddenly it came to her.

Getting to her feet she told Helen, 'I'm going up to Mum's study. I want to look at what she was working on last night.'

Gran, pouring the water down the sink, looked over her shoulder. 'Are you sure you're up to it?' She set the upturned basin on the draining board. 'Simon will be here soon. He's bringing a team from MI5, they'll have the best minds in the country working on this.'

Maya stood up. 'I know. But none of them cares about Mum as much as I do.'

Entering her mum's study was shattering. Pam's laptop was on her desk, just as it had been the night before. With difficulty, because of her bandaged hand, Maya managed to open it up and log on.

Recent documents

Immediately she spotted something interesting. A file – *Red Moon*.

She tried to open it. *Access denied*. She tried

another route but didn't succeed. Damn! It must be the file Mum was working on last night, and she was sure there was crucial stuff in it, information linked to the kidnapping.

Think, Maya, think.

It was hard getting her brain to function, her head felt like it was stuffed full of cotton wool, she couldn't focus. What had Pam said last night? Her eyes fell on a red file at the side of the computer. On the cover, in Pam's handwriting, was written, 'Circle of Fire.' With a banging heart she flipped it open. It was empty – but the title stuck in her brain. Of course! Fire! That was it, the password – *Firecracker*. She typed in the word and opened the file.

Red Moon

Islamic fundamentalist cells are not operating individually but are linked throughout Europe. Their mission is to perpetrate a summer of burning – in their words, to ring Europe in a 'Circle of Fire'. A series of attacks on major European cities is planned. The first will probably take place in England, followed by more attacks on public buildings in all major cities. Intelligence tells us that the first attack, possibly planned for the north of England, is imminent. . .

Her mind exploded. This was massive. Mum had

collected loads of data – surveillance reports, dates of meetings, code words, suspects. It must be the report she was going to present to the Counter Terrorism unit she headed – code name, *Viper*.

Maya scrolled down the information Pam had collated: names of organisations, dates of meetings, a list of movements and destinations – Amsterdam, Madrid, Pakistan. There were photos too, rows of mug-shots, mainly men with beards, most of them young, and a few girls, wearing headscarves.

At the bottom of one paragraph Pam had typed, *Source – Khaled Husain. Meeting 3.30 p.m. June 4th*.

Maya sat back. June 4th – today! So, he was the informant she was meeting in Leeds – Khaled Husain. Pam had said she trusted him, but wasn't it a strange coincidence that on the very day of their meeting she'd been kidnapped? Was he a double agent who'd betrayed Pam? When her mum gave her the password, had she known something might go wrong? Friend or enemy, he was a crucial player.

She'd tell Simon, he had to find Khaled Husain.

Chapter Four

The black jeep was speeding south. The men were silent, following instructions. In the back seat Pamela was wedged between two of them, hands tied behind her, eyes blindfolded, mouth gagged with tape. It was uncomfortable, but they hadn't hurt her, and they hadn't taken Maya. Poor love, how horrible for her – Pam imagined the panic, the fear that would cut to the bone.

Remember the password, Maya. Open the Red Moon file. Tell Simon he must contact Khaled. Go to the bookshop, find Khaled.

Pam was concentrating so hard on sending Maya a mind message that she jumped when a voice burst from a short wave radio. Some sort of code word was given and the driver swung the jeep sharply to the left. In the back, an injured man moaned with every jolt.

The noise of other traffic faded as they travelled over what Pam thought were country lanes with lots of twists and turns and then, finally, the jeep bumped into a ditch and drove over a deeply rutted road. It was some sort of work depot or a farm track, Pam guessed.

She was right about the farm. The jeep stopped in front of a gate. There was a short pause while it was opened and shut and then they drove up to an old farmhouse surrounded by derelict sheds and a crumbling barn.

When the car door opened, Pam smelt an acrid scent of old bricks and lime, mixed with the stink of manure. The men on either side of her moved away and got out. Car doors slammed. She heard them unloading the man from the back; he cried out in pain.

'Careful, careful with him,' a voice ordered.

Squeezing her shoulder blades together, Pam reared back against the seat, trying to wriggle her wrists free of the tight binding. Her training told her she should cooperate with the kidnappers, her instinct told her to escape.

A hand touched her shoulder. 'Stay cool,' a voice said. 'Don't make trouble and you won't get hurt.'

The voice was young and male. He had a marked northern accent. He gripped her arm and started to pull her sideways. Pam didn't resist. When her feet touched the ground, she lurched forward. A strong hand steadied her.

As they marched forward, Pam blinked and wrinkled her nose, trying to see under the blindfold but it was too thick and securely tied. She was led across some rough ground and up two steps, then her captor paused.

'Take her inside,' a deep voice ordered.

She was pushed into what smelt like an old, damp house. Bare floorboards creaked under her feet, footsteps echoed through empty rooms. There were other people around – more footsteps, shuffling and whispering. It was unnerving not being able to see. The man guiding her shoved her down onto a hard chair.

It was important not to lose her nerve, to keep her dignity. She wished she wasn't in her running clothes, and that she was wearing something that covered more of her body than the tight vest and small pink shorts. But how many times had she told recruits,

'If you behave like a victim, you'll become one'?

So, with all the resources she could muster, she said in a commanding voice, 'I'm cold. I need a blanket.'

Her appeal was ignored. Footsteps retreated, voices rose from another room – they were arguing, one person loud and accusing. Pam edged off the chair and shuffled forward to listen.

'Why don't we get rid of her now?'

'No! You know Omar's orders.'

The next words were lost as the voices became a low murmur. Then a sharp, high, questioning voice rose. 'So, what do we do with her?'

'Move her when it's dark,' came the reply.

There was a brief silence, then some muttering, followed by footsteps creaking into the room.

'Sit down!' somebody yelled.

Strong hands took hold of Pam's shoulders, dragging her back to the chair. The young man with the northern accent spoke to her. 'Somebody'll bring you fresh clothes. There'll be a woman to attend to yer.'

'What do you want?' Pam asked, as calmly as she could.

'We want you to cooperate with us.'

Pam sat up straight. 'Why should I do that?'

There was a slight pause, a sniff. 'You asked us not to take your daughter. We were merciful. But remember, we know where she is. If you don't do as we ask, we'll cut her throat.'

Pam's heart froze. Desperate words echoed in her head.

Please not Maya, this is nothing to do with her. Leave Maya alone. This is my work, my battle.

'What do you want me to do?' she asked.

'You'll find out soon enough.'

'Could you please untie the blindfold? It's very hard talking to somebody I can't see.'

For a moment nobody spoke. Pam waited, hoping they'd agree.

'All right,' the young man with the northern accent said.

The scarf was untied, and Pam stared into a bare, dimly-lit room. The windows had been blanked out so that the three figures standing at some distance were just shadows.

Pam turned round and looked up, hoping to see the person who'd uncovered her eyes. 'Thank you,' she said.

The man moved quickly away, but she caught

sight of his small, stocky figure dressed in black. He snatched up a chair and dragged it across the floorboards to sit in front of her; this time he was close enough for Pam to see his face. He was young, his cheeks round and smooth – a chubby, friendly-looking face, framed by a black hood.

'So, who's giving you your information?' he said, with a forced smile.

Pam gazed directly at him, her eyes unflinching. 'What do you mean?' she asked.

The young man's nose twitched, his lip curled; he had a gap between his two front teeth. As he spoke, his benign manner changed; he spat out his words, his eyes went cold as dagger blades. 'We're not stupid, we know you've got agents tagging us – somebody's squealing. One of our brothers is betraying us. We want his name.'

Pam answered coolly but pleasantly. 'I don't know what you're talking about.'

The man made a snorting noise. He lifted his head and his hood fell back, allowing Pam to see the silver streak of a deep scar across the top of his forehead. 'Well, it's early days yet,' he snapped.

He got up, went round the back of her chair and grabbed a handful of hair. A searing pain tore through

Pam's scalp, but she stifled her screams.

'Don't worry, you'll squeal before we've done with yer,' he laughed. 'You won't need much persuadin'.'

'Don't touch my daughter,' Pam gasped. 'Please leave her alone.'

The man stepped back. 'Her fate is in your hands.'

Pam was left trembling as her tormentor moved away, his footsteps fading. Outside the room, the man pulled off the black hood and faced the others. He was young, in his early twenties at most. Scratching his head, he brushed aside his short dark hair.

'Right, I'm reporting back to Omar,' he told the other guys. 'You've got your orders. When you get the word, move 'er up north.' He jiggled his shoulders, a restless movement, showing he was anxious to be off. 'Leave the jeep in the barn an' use the BMW. Don't take any chances, shove her in the boot.'

He pulled a piece of paper from his pocket. 'In one hour she phones her daughter, right? This is what she's gotta say – only these words, nothin' else.'

One of the hooded men took it, read it

and nodded. 'OK.'

The young man with the scarred forehead was about to go, when he squared his shoulders and faced the Brothers. 'That bitch thought she was gonna to upset all our plans. Well, she was wrong. Western armies are occupying our lands – now, we're bringing terror to Europe.'

Turning his back on them, he swaggered through the farmyard, black hood dangling from his hand. He opened the door of a red truck and climbed inside.

'It's war,' he muttered, as he sped away.

Chapter Five

The helicopter landed in the back field, swirling up clouds of leaves and dust and hay. Maya watched a tall man in jeans and a dark jacket dodge under the whirling blades. Moments later, as she stood in the kitchen with her arm round Helen, the same man walked in through the back door.

'I'm Simon Maundsley,' he said. 'I came as quickly as I could.'

'Thank you,' Helen said, holding out her hand to him.

He shook her hand and then looked at Maya. 'How are you?' he asked. His voice was warm, full of concern but his blue eyes were sharp, taking in everything.

'I'm OK,' Maya said.

She didn't look OK, Simon thought – she looked pale and shaken. But he had a job to do. 'Good,' he said. 'Because I'm going to need your help. I want you to tell me every detail.'

This man who'd descended like Superman was quite a surprise to Maya. Good-looking, his blond hair streaked and spiky, and much younger than Maya had expected. But she wasn't interested in his looks, she only hoped he was as good at his job as Pam had said he was.

'I need to organise a search at the place where Pam was seized,' Simon said. 'Can you show my men where it was?'

Maya clasped her hands, twisting her fingers, panic flashing across her face. 'I don't want to go back there. They had guns. I keep seeing pictures, hearing stuff – screaming, shooting.' She touched her bloody lip, closed her eyes and breathed deeply, trying to calm herself. 'I can't go back yet. Poor Danny; lying there under the hedge, just lying there – dead. It's horrible.'

Helen gently massaged Maya's sore shoulder. 'Oh, my love,' she murmured.

'Has she seen a doctor?' Simon asked.

Maya glared at him. 'I don't want a doctor.

I'm all right. I'm not going to collapse in a heap. I want to help. I just don't feel able to go back to the lane, not yet, but if I've got to, if it'll help Mum, I'll do it.'

'It's all right,' Simon said. 'It might be more use if you stay here.' Taking off his jacket, he set down his briefcase. 'As long as somebody can guide my men.'

'I'll take them,' Helen said.

'There should be some local cops there. Hope they haven't ruined the evidence. And Forensics should be along soon,' he said. Unzipping his briefcase, he searched through some documents and pulled out a sheet of paper. 'Can you go now?'

Helen darted a worried glance at Maya. 'Will you be all right?'

'Yeah.' Maya said. 'I'll be fine.'

'Come here.' Helen folded Maya in her arms. 'Stay strong, my love. Stay strong for Pam.'

Maya felt some of her gran's strength flowing into her. There *was* hope, she must hope, she had to believe everything was going to be all right.

Simon went to talk to two men hovering at the back door. He handed one of them the sheet of paper he'd pulled from his briefcase. 'Give this to Forensics. It's authorisation for a thorough examination of the site. I want swabs and samples, a full report. Tell them this investigation has top priority.'

After giving Maya a last hug, Helen picked up her keys and bag and went out to her car, followed by the two men.

'Right,' Simon said, as soon as Helen's car started up. 'Let's get to work. I want you tell me everything you remember.'

'From the beginning?' Maya asked.

'Yes. From the beginning.'

An officer who'd been hovering on the back drive was brought in. Simon introduced her as Olivia Shears and began setting up equipment to record Maya's words.

Sitting at the kitchen table, Maya found it hard to keep her mind focused. She patiently described every traumatic detail, but she wanted action – she imagined leaping into the helicopter, sweeping over the countryside, scouring lanes and major roads. She'd expected hi-tech equipment and sat disconsolately while Simon made notes in a book.

'Is anybody out there? Is anybody actually looking for Mum?' she asked.

Simon puffed out his cheeks and raised his eyebrows. 'I've put out a call on the Mercedes, relayed a description of the jeep to all units. The crime site's been cordoned off – Forensics should be down there now. As soon as there's any news, HQ will contact me.' He looked at Maya's anxious face and said gently, 'Your mum doesn't operate on her own, you know. She heads a team – a crack team of specially trained intelligence agents linked to MI5, MI6. All units will be involved in recovering her. Trust me, everything that can be done is being done. We won't let her down, everybody wants her found.'

Maya planted her elbows on the table and fixed him with a steely glare. 'Not as much as I do,' she said.

Simon blinked, looked as if he was going to say something more, then put his head down and added to his notes. When he'd finished, he looked up. 'Can you remember anything about the men's voices?' he asked. 'Any accent at all?'

Maya flicked at a crumb on the table. 'Northern. You need to find Khaled Husain.'

'Where did you get that name?' Simon asked, with surprise.

Sitting forward, Maya gazed levelly into Simon's pale blue eyes. 'Mum was going up to Leeds this afternoon to meet an informant. I'm pretty sure it was Khaled Husain. She said he'd got something vital to tell her – the one last piece of information she needed.'

'Pam told you this?'

'Yes. And she gave me a password to log on to her computer.'

Simon turned away, biting his lip. 'She must have thought she was in danger. Why didn't she inform me?' He picked up his briefcase. 'Where's Pam's laptop?'

'Upstairs.'

Maya led the way, followed by Simon and Olivia.

'Are you sure you're all right?' Olivia asked Maya, as they climbed the stairs.

'Yeah, I'm coping,' Maya said, glancing back at her. 'I'm trying not to think about this morning, blanking it – I want to keep my mind clear, help as much as I can.'

'Well, you're doing great,' Olivia told her. 'Your mum would be proud.'

The remark nearly poleaxed Maya but stoically she opened the door into her mum's room and became very businesslike, plugging in the laptop, typing in the password and accessing the Red Moon file.

'My God!' Simon murmured. 'This is incredible.' He covered his mouth with his hand, breathing heavily. 'This shows the whole picture – it proves that all the small individual Islamist cells we've been tracking, they're linked, just as we suspected, they're part of an international network.' He leaned forward for a closer look. 'And they want to blow up the whole bloody world!'

'Mum had almost cracked it,' Maya said. 'One more day and she'd have sorted it – alerted all units, got things moving.'

'Did the Brotherhood know that? Did somebody betray her?' Simon muttered.

Maya pointed to Khaled's photo. 'Could have been him. Mum said she trusted him, but on the day she was due to meet him, she's taken hostage. Coincidence, or what?'

'Certainly something to think about,' Simon said.'

Maya looked up at him. 'So, what're you going to do?'

He took a moment, staring out of the window, his face furrowed with thought, then he came round the desk and knelt on the floor, his hand gripping the edge of the desk, his knuckles white. He leaned forward, his face level with Maya's. 'At the moment I'm not sure. If this Khaled is a double agent, we need to proceed carefully. They'll know one hell of a lot about us.'

'But it's obvious, the Allied Brotherhood are the people who've kidnapped Mum. You arrest Khaled Husain, talk to him, break him down. He's the one who can lead you to Mum, he's the one who can stop the bombs.'

Simon turned away staring into the distance.

Maya's voice became more shrill. 'You've got to round these people up – they're terrorists.' She pushed back her chair and shot him a challenging glare.

'I understand how you feel,' Simon said. 'But tackling an organised group like this takes planning. We have to build a case, find evidence and make sure we get all of them, not just the foot soldiers but the leaders too.'

'But if you wait, they'll plant their bombs and they'll hurt Mum.'

'You have to trust me,' Simon said. 'We proceed with care – it's the way your mum would do things. We have to keep an open mind.' He levered himself up and straightened his jacket. 'We've been tracking other terrorist cells who could have carried out the kidnapping – a group wanting publicity for their cause or any terrorist organisation wanting to use Pam to bargain with the government. We can't go jumping to conclusions.'

'But it must be them,' Maya said, gesturing to the photos on the screen. 'They knew she was getting close, knew she was going to expose them – that's why they've kidnapped her.'

Simon leaned back, his eyes half-closed, thinking. Maya fiddled irritably with her mum's pen, clicking the ball point in and out.

'It's a credible theory. Whether these would-be terrorists have your mum or not, they need to be stopped. I'll set up a surveillance team to monitor the bookshop.'

'So, you mean, we just wait?'

Simon nodded. 'I have to warn you,' he said, 'when a hostage's taken, it's a waiting game. At the moment, the kidnappers think they hold all the cards. We have to be patient until they show their hand – then we can act.' He folded his arms. 'I know it's not want you want to hear, but being cautious, psyching them out, is the most effective and safest way to get a hostage back alive.'

As he spoke, Maya gazed at the computer screen,

her eyes focused on Khaled Husain. His features blurred, his green eyes floated and seemed to come to life, his gaze was piercing. She couldn't explain it but it was as if he was sending her a message, as if he knew her. Was he an enemy or a friend?

* * *

In her room Maya stood with her back against the door, twisting the silver and ruby ring Mum had given her for her fourteenth birthday.

Please Mum, don't be difficult. Do as they say, stay alive.

Going over to the window, she saw two police cars blocking off the bottom of the drive – she wasn't sure whether that made her feel safe or scared. The throbbing sound of a helicopter came close as it circled over the woods – more surveillance.

In the middle of the bed Maya's mobile phone winked accusingly. She picked it up, cursing again that she hadn't taken it along on the run. Scrolling down her list of contacts she tapped in Pam's number, but of course it was dead. Somehow it made her feel better to keep on trying, so she tapped on Pam's name over and over again, but every time it failed to connect.

She threw the phone on the bed as the helicopter came clattering back. Through the window, she watched it swoop across the valley, circle the cottage and disappear over the hill. Her eyes scanned down to the woods. Simon had warned her to be careful, not to leave the house or even go outside. Was there still somebody out there? A worm of terror wriggled down her back.

Throwing herself on the bed she lay face down, drumming on the mattress with her feet. Flashing pictures invaded her mind and she heard a voice, Danny's voice, trying to save her, shouting the warning, 'Keep Down! Down!' It was on repeat, bouncing and echoing round her brain. Rolling from side to side she hugged her knees; although it was hot and sunny outside she felt suddenly chilled. She touched her grazed cheek, her bloody lip, and shivered. Perhaps Simon had been right, perhaps the doctor should have come out to see her, but she didn't want tranquillisers, she wanted action.

Slipping under the duvet, she rubbed her arms, then started to bite at a fingernail poking out from the bandage. She hated herself. She'd done nothing to help Pam; she'd just stood there and watched them take her away. The pictures came again in vivid detail. Her common sense told her she could have done nothing effective against five men with guns, but she couldn't stop picking at the scene. She was driving herself mad, she had to calm down.

Simon had told her there was nothing to do but wait. A special meeting of Viper had been called. The country was on Critical Alert. There were teams collecting evidence and when there was news, he'd let her know.

I have to be ready, I can't just lie here, Maya thought. If anything happens, I have to be ready to go.

Leaping out of bed, she darted across the room, reached into the back of a cupboard and pulled out a basket. Lifting it up she ran into the bathroom and locked the door. The basket was loaded with toiletries – Christmas presents never unwrapped. A tangle of citrus and flowers filled her nose as she opened the packages.

She gathered bottles and boxes into her arms, unwound the bandage from her hand and dashed into the shower. Stepping into the cascading water she soaped and lathered, shampooed and buffed and tried to put every negative thought out of her head.

There was still hope, they hadn't shot Pam. It would have been easy to do it there in the quiet lane, but they didn't, so that meant they wanted her alive.

In her room, she pulled underwear out of the drawer and was just about to put it on when she suddenly changed her mind. She rummaged underneath and found a lovely set of never-worn black lace underwear with scarlet flowers, a new Elle T-shirt and her best Miss Sixty jeans, all bought for her by Pam on their last shopping trip.

I love you Mum. Hang on, don't despair. We'll find you.

Towelling her hair dry, Maya smoothed in some oil and plugged in the hairdryer. When she flicked the switch, the TV came on as well. Pictures of a Palestinian school bus blasted by an Israeli missile filled the screen. There was a close-up of a child's shoe, a backpack and torn teddy bear. She couldn't stand it, and flicked channels to a morning chat show. A girl with blonde hair and big boobs – which she was proudly displaying in a very low-cut tight dress – was talking about how a stint on a reality TV show had given her enough money to re-model her body.

Maya couldn't bear that either. Flicking to another station, she gulped as a different face filled the screen; someone with naturally blonde hair, lovely grey eyes and sweet freckles on her nose – her mum. She switched off the hairdryer.

We interrupt this programme with a newsflash.

News is just coming in that Pamela Brown, newly appointed Head of a government Counter Terrorism unit, has been seized by an armed gang.

Ms Brown was out running in a Derbyshire village when she was grabbed by masked gunmen. Special Forces agents fired back at the gang. A security agent was killed but Ms Brown's daughter escaped unharmed. Police are trying to trace a black jeep with red upholstery and tinted windows which is believed to be travelling south.

Maya clasped her hands as the camera zoomed in on the cottage and then showed the spot where Mum was abducted. She stared at the screen, her mouth open. The world had stopped.

Mum, where are you?

Chapter Six

'How're you feeling?' Simon asked, as Maya walked into the kitchen.

She couldn't answer. There were no words.

'Oh, you've changed,' he said, glancing up from the wires he was connecting. 'Good idea, fresh clothes. Your gran will be back in a minute. She's been keeping the neighbours at bay down on the lane.'

Maya nodded. 'OK. Fine.'

The kitchen had been turned into a computer lab, nothing looked familiar any more; wires, aerials, monitors, hard drives and metal boxes cluttered the kitchen table.

'Did you find anything else on Mum's laptop?' Maya asked, plonking herself down beside a monitor that was screening a view of the front gate.

'Yep. Useful stuff,' Simon answered. 'I've got people working on it.'

Maya watched as he tested levers and switches. Was he really the whiz-kid Pam thought he was? She wanted to ask him if there was any news of the jeep, but his mobile went off and he disappeared into the hall, closing the door behind him.

Staring out at the garden, Maya saw the sun was still shining; the weather was beautiful. She leaned her aching head on her hands. It was torture, just sitting doing nothing, but she didn't seem to be able to move. On one of the monitors she saw TV news vans and reporters arriving at the bottom of the drive. The gate opened and a car came through. A few minutes later the car arrived on the back drive and Helen got out, followed by two agents.

'Any news?' Helen asked as she came in.

Maya lifted her head. 'No. A few phone calls, people offering to help, but there's nothing anybody can do at the moment.'

'No, I suppose not,' Helen said.

'Did the investigators find anything down at the lane?'

'Tyre marks, spent cartridges. Hope they can

make something of it.'

Helen's body was stiff, her face tense and strained. Slowly she went over to the sink and washed her hands. Then, abruptly, she went into a flurry of activity, tidying the kitchen and making food. She asked Maya if she wanted a sandwich. Maya refused; she was too miserable to eat, and instead, she sat idly picking at the new bandage she'd wrapped round her hand.

The hall door opened and Simon walked in with a look of triumph on his face. 'They've traced the jeep. It's at a farmhouse in Hertfordshire, just north of London. They think Pam's inside the building.'

Maya's heart leapt in hope.

'I've ordered all units there,' Simon added.

'Are we going in?' Olivia asked.

'Not yet. We don't know what ammo they've got. We surround them, then we wait – try and psyche them out.'

Helen dropped the knife she was holding and started to shake. Maya went over to her. 'It'll be all right, Gran, it'll be all right.'

She led Helen to a chair and sat her down. 'They won't hurt Mum, will they?' she asked Simon, her eyes pleading.

Simon glanced at her, then averted his eyes. He didn't say anything and Maya knew he couldn't. Nobody knew what was going to happen.

'Do you think the kidnappers will try and bargain?' she asked.

'Possibly,' Simon answered. 'But don't get too hopeful. Government policy is strictly no deals with terrorists.'

His words thumped into Maya as if he'd punched her. 'What?' she demanded. 'If we can't make a deal, how the hell is Mum going to be set free?'

Olivia looked up from the keyboard she was using. 'We have a skilled negotiating team. They'll wear them down.'

'And if that fails?' Helen asked.

'Then we'll have to send in a team of firearms officers,' Olivia said.

'You mean, blast the place apart?' Maya asked incredulously.

'Let's hope it won't come to that,' Simon said.

'You're not giving me much hope,' Maya said angrily. 'The government won't bargain; the kidnappers might shoot her! But if Mum does survive, chances are she'll die in the rescue operation. Great!'

'Maya!' Helen called but Maya didn't stop as

she ran out of the kitchen and up into the bathroom. Her legs were like straw, her stomach was in her throat. A wave of sickness overwhelmed her. Closing her eyes, she had an image of her mum tied up, her face scared in a way she'd never seen it before. She hung over the sink and splashed her face with cold water.

Breathing in quickly and sharply, she stared at herself in the mirror. She looked grim, her mouth puckered into a thin slash of crimson, lines etched on her forehead, a haunted look in her eyes – a dark ghost.

* * *

Pam moved her shoulders and neck, trying to ease the stiffness. She'd been sitting in the same position – ankles bound to the crude wooden chair, hands tied behind her back, mouth taped up – for what seemed like hours. Earlier, a woman had brought her a pair of long black trousers and an oversized black T-shirt that hung almost to her knees, so at least she wasn't cold, but every time she moved, the bindings bit into her ankles and wrists. How long would they leave her like this? What were they going to do with her?

She listened intently to every sound and heard a car engine, the clang of metal, the scuffing of heavy sacks or boxes being pulled across the floor. Then footsteps rapped on the floorboards outside, the door opened and two people came into the room, – not the small, stocky man who'd seemed to be in charge, but a tall, thin man and a woman. The room was so dim that she could only see their outlines, but the tall thin man came towards her, put his hands on either side of her head then ripped the tape from her mouth.

'Thank you,' Pam said, although her lips were stinging so much, it hurt to speak.

The man drew out a sharp knife. Pam gulped and shuddered as he bent down, his beard close to her face. For a moment she stared into his cold eyes, then he pushed her shoulders forward and leaned down to cut the binding from her hands.

Straightening her arms, she rubbed at her sore wrists. The woman, dressed in jeans, black T-shirt and black headscarf, set down a tray and offered Pam a plate of food. 'Please eat,' she said.

Pam waved the food away – she wasn't hungry.

'You must eat something. It might be a long

time before you get anything again,' the young woman said.

'Why?' Pam asked.

'You're going to be moved.'

'Where are you taking me?' Pam asked.

'That's none of your business,' the man butted in. He motioned towards the plate of food with his knife. 'Eat,' he said.

Pam thought she'd better humour them, so, taking the plate, she placed it on her lap, spooned up a bit of rice and chewed. It was soggy and tasteless and made her feel sick.

'I can't eat this,' she said.

The young woman leaned forward. 'Two more spoonfuls,' she said, quite gently, as one would bargain with a child.

Obediently, Pam ate two more spoonfuls of the grey rice. Then she handed back the plate.

Immediately the tall bearded man waved a mobile phone at her. It was hers – the one they'd taken from her.

'Before you leave here, you can phone your daughter. Tell her you're safe,' he said.

Pam had to clench her fists to stop herself from snatching the phone. She longed to hear Maya's voice, and if she phoned the cottage they'd get a trace on the call. She reached for the phone, but before she could take it the man grabbed her wrist, his fingers digging painfully into her flesh.

'Wait a moment,' he snapped. 'You say only this. Read it!'

He pulled the phone away and held up a piece of paper scrawled with big letters.

'I can't see it properly,' Pam said quietly.

'Here.' The woman shone a torch onto the paper.

In a quivering voice Pam read the words aloud. 'This is Pamela Brown. I'm not hurt or injured. If no attempt is made to find me and no suspects are rounded up, the Brotherhood will state their terms for my release. I repeat: do not try and find me. Do not arrest any Muslim brothers. We will contact you again in three days.'

As she finished reading, she was aware of the bearded man staring at her with hatred. 'If you say anything else, add anything at all, your daughter will suffer.'

* * *

Slamming into her bedroom, Maya had a major stress

attack, pacing up and down, thumping the furniture, kicking the wall. Finally exhausted, she fell onto the bed and lay looking up at the ceiling. If Pam was a prisoner in the farmhouse, what would happen to her? Please let her be OK, she prayed.

Rolling onto her side she stared up at the tattered target pinned to her noticeboard – a souvenir from the birthday treat at the Training Academy. Just two months ago, when she'd shot out the middle of the target and roared round the driving circuit, she'd had no idea that her life was about to take such a dark turn. Pam had been so proud of her that day. If only she could put her skills to use and do something to help.

Down in the hall the phone was ringing. The three house phones had been going all morning, so Maya didn't take much notice. Next moment, though, she was fully alert. Somebody was screaming her name and footsteps came running up the stairs. When Olivia burst in, Maya was already at the bedroom door.

Olivia grabbed her arm. 'It's Pam. Quick! Down in the kitchen.'

Before Olivia had finished speaking, Maya was ahead of her, racing down the stairs and flying into the kitchen. She picked up the receiver lying on the worktop.

'Mum!'

She jammed the phone to her ear, her body shaking with excitement. Simon had flicked a switch to tape the call, and he watched as Maya listened. For a few seconds he saw Maya straight-backed, focused, then her shoulders sagged, her head drooped and she shouted desperately three times, 'Mum, Mum, Mum!'

Helen moved in quickly. 'What did she say, darling? What did she say?'

Maya's mouth was slack with shock. Her eyes stared without seeing.

'She told me to look for the moon.'

Chapter Seven

Maya held onto the worktop. Her thoughts were all over the place. She stared at the necklace Helen was wearing – three strands of soft, milky-white pearls. 'Mum wants me to go to Leeds,' she said. 'She wants me to go to the bookshop.'

'Did she say that?' Simon asked.

'She told me to look for the moon.'

'That's what Pam always said when she was leaving, when you were little and she was away a lot, don't you remember?' Helen said, gently. 'You both promised to look up at the moon and think about each other.'

'I know,' Maya said. 'But this time it was more than that. I know it was. What she said – it wasn't like Mum; her words were flat as if she were reading them. Then just at the end, just before somebody snatched the phone away, she whispered, "Look for the moon". She said it urgently. It was a message, a secret message.'

Three pairs of eyes stared at her.

'Mum knew I'd understand,' Maya told them. 'And I do. I know what she was asking me to do – to go to the bookshop, the Red Moon bookshop.'

Simon's eyebrows shot up. He smoothed his hand over his spiky hair.

'I see the connection,' he said. 'But Pam wouldn't ask you to do anything so dangerous.'

Maya glared at him. 'Mum trusts me.'

'I'm sure she does, but even so.' He left the words hanging in the air as he pulled the tape recorder towards him. 'Let's listen to the message,' he suggested. 'See if there's any background noise, anything we can pick up.'

They all sat down at the table and listened to Pam's voice. For Maya and Helen it was heartbreaking. Pam's words were tense and expressionless. Then came the breathless instruction uttered at the end of the message, 'Maya, look for the moon,' whispered quickly before someone pulled the phone away and cut her off.

The face of Khaled Husain swam before Maya's eyes, his green eyes hypnotic, as if beckoning her. She had a strong sense that she had to talk to him. She had to know if he'd betrayed Pam, or if he was loyal. Whichever it was, she was sure he held the key to finding her.

She was so preoccupied that it took a moment before she registered what Olivia was saying.

'. . . an echoing, empty space – an empty building, an old building, I would imagine.'

'Yes,' Simon agreed. 'And did you pick up the sound of dripping water? Let's get the sound people working on it. See what else they can come up with.'

'I'll make a copy and get it to them,' Olivia said.

'Hm,' Simon said. 'It fits with the empty farm building. The helicopter should be back in a few minutes. I need to get down there and coordinate operations.'

'So, are you sending anybody up to Leeds?' Maya asked.

'No need,' Simon said, reaching for his jacket. 'There's already a surveillance team up there. They know about the bookshop.'

Maya's mind was buzzing. 'So, you can get somebody to track him – arrest Khaled Husain.'

Simon's face wrinkled. 'We don't want to arrest anybody at the moment. The balance is precarious. Let's see what develops.'

'I'm sure Mum's in Leeds,' she said. 'The kidnappers had northern accents. They could have moved her into a different car. They could have deliberately confused you.'

Simon picked up his briefcase. 'I'm perfectly aware of that, but there are other things linking the kidnap to the farmhouse. I have to go,' he said.

'Then I want to come with you,' Maya said, getting up.

'That's out of the question.'

'Why?'

'Because I don't know what's going to happen.'

'Then let me go up to Leeds. I could speak to this Khaled guy. Nobody would suspect me.'

Simon shook his head. 'That's not possible, Maya. Your mother would never forgive me if I put you in danger.'

'Where's the danger? You just told me Pam's not been taken north, that she's in the farmhouse. I'd just be talking to a guy.'

'And what if he's the one who betrayed Pam?' Simon asked her. 'No, we have specially trained agents to do this sort of work.'

'But I could go now,' Maya said determinedly. 'Olivia could take me. Mum wouldn't have sent me a message if she didn't want me to find Khaled and talk to him.'

Simon shook his head. 'No, Maya. I think you misunderstood.'

'But she knows . . . she knows she can trust me. And she knows I'll be desperate to help, so she's giving me something to do. Don't you see? And I'm Muslim. Well, my family was. It wouldn't be dangerous because they'd think I was one of them. She wants me to go and speak to Khaled Husain, I know she does.'

Simon bit his lip and winced. 'The best thing you can do for your mum is stay here and stay safe. She may contact you again – her message gave us three days.'

Maya was only half-listening, she was looking into the distance, her lips pressed together, biting at her nails. 'Mum told me,' she whispered. 'She wanted me to go.'

'I have to leave,' Simon said, putting on his jacket. Picking up Pam's laptop he turned to Helen. 'We'll let you know the minute there's any news.'

They watched him go across the garden, slip through the hedge and stride across the back field towards the helicopter.

Maya felt he was deserting them, and hope drained away as he disappeared from sight. She wasn't sure he'd really listened to her, treated what she'd said seriously enough.

'I'm going up to my room,' she told Gran.

'Why don't you stay down here? I'll make us all a cup of tea,' Olivia suggested.

'Yes,' Helen said, 'that would be nice.'

'I want to be on my own for a while,' Maya said.

Slowly she climbed the stairs, went into her room and locked the door behind her. Sitting down at the desk she reached into the back of a cupboard and pulled out her laptop, then she bent to open a drawer. Copying Pam's files had been smart, the one good move she'd made, and she congratulated herself as she slotted in the disk. Elbows on the desk, she propped her head on her hand, stared at the photo of Khaled Husain and re-read her mum's words – *Khaled Husain, Manager of the Red Moon bookshop.*

It was true that when she was little and Pam's work had taken her overseas, they'd had an understanding that wherever Pam was, she'd look up at the moon and think about Maya, and from her bedroom window Maya would do the same. One snowy night, the night before her eighth birthday Maya had been in their London apartment staring at the moon hanging above the city skyline, hoping her mum would be back in time to help her celebrate. It would be easy to think that was what Pam had been remembering – but Maya knew it was something more.

Scrolling down the report she read:

A group in Leeds calling themselves the Allied Brotherhood are the English cell of Red Moon. Self-styled leader of the AB is Omar Hamed.

Maya's mind flicked back. She pictured the driver of the silver Mercedes. She was certain he'd been watching her and Pam, waiting for them to reach a pre-arranged spot so that he could alert his men. It surely wasn't a coincidence that he'd driven past and scared them just before the jeep arrived.

*Operation Red Moon is a plot to blow up major public attractions at weekly intervals in important European cities this summer. When the code word is given, their plan will be put into operation. The * marked characters are pledged suicide bombers.*

Maya's blood ran cold as she scanned the rows of photographs. She was sure these were the people who'd captured Pam. Bombings, shootings, beheadings – every gory picture she'd ever seen in the newspapers and on TV bloomed in her head. When she looked again at Khaled's picture, she saw it was marked with an asterisk. Just as before, his eyes seemed to be telling her something. Did he know where Pam was? Was he a friend or an enemy?

She leaned forward, scrolled down the screen and studied the other photos. Men with beards, mostly young, some wearing tight black caps, a couple with long hair under baseball caps. A few women, their heads covered, their eyes dark and unsmiling. Twelve photos marked with an asterisk – nine young men and three women willing to die for their cause.

Maya's eyes flicked over them, and one image in particular caught her attention – a man with a round podgy face who was almost smiling, his nose broad, a gap in his front teeth – but the most distinctive feature on his face was a scar across his forehead. She leaned closer, staring. It was him! One of the guys who'd grabbed her. She'd glimpsed the scar under his hood. It was unmistakable.

A deep shudder ran through her. Gripping the edge of her desk she closed her eyes. In the distance she heard the helicopter taking off from the back field.

Simon was on his way to the farmhouse, but here in front of her was evidence to show it was the Leeds group who'd captured Pam. Simon was heading in the wrong direction.

Her mum's words echoed in her head. *Look for the moon, Maya.* As she twisted the ring on her finger, her mind was flooded with sounds and pictures. Ear-shattering gunfire, the spatter of gravel, blood, thick and dark, draining life, glistening on grass.

She squeezed her hands together, saw a cellar, stone-cold and dark. A family in hiding, a little girl clinging to her mother's hand. From outside came the crack of rifles, the shouts of a crazed mob. Huddled together, the family waited. Finally the firing stopped. A door opened, footsteps thumped down the stairs.

That was the last time she saw her family. Pam had rescued her. She owed her life to Pam; now it was time to honour that debt.

Chapter Eight

Working quickly and quietly, Maya grabbed a small rucksack and threw in her mobile and some basic clothes: a fresh pair of jeans, knickers, a couple of tops. Skidding into the bathroom she scooped up toothbrush and toothpaste, caught sight of her face in the mirror, wiped a smear of blood from her upper lip and smoothed a dab of concealer over a graze on her cheek. From the hook on her door she picked up a jacket, put it on and was ready. Looking out of the window, she spotted two security guards on the back lawn and a host of TV cameras and journalists at the gate. Somehow she had to get out of the house without being seen.

Money! Scooting over to her desk, she snatched her purse out of the drawer, made sure her bank card was in it and shoved it in the zip compartment of her rucksack. Hoisting the rucksack onto her shoulder, she tiptoed over to the door and listened. Somebody was coming up the stairs.

There was a light knock on her door.

'Maya? It's Gran. Are you all right?'

She slipped back the bolt and put her head round the edge of the door. 'Is there any news?'

'No, nothing yet,' Helen answered.

Maya sighed. 'I'll come down soon. I just want to be on my own for a while.'

'All right, darling.'

She listened to Gran's footsteps fading and going downstairs. A pang of guilt struck her – if she left the house, she'd cause Helen more worry. But she had to go. She couldn't just sit around and wait three days – she had to do something.

Snatching up a notepad, she scribbled a quick note to Helen and left it on her pillow. *Don't worry Gran. I'll be back soon.* Then, tiptoeing along the landing she glanced over the banister into the hall below. There was nobody there, but spotting the cellar door gave her a great idea – a short tunnel led from the cellar to the old ice house in the back garden.

Blood racing, nerves trembling, Maya crept down

the stairs. At the end of the hallway she wrenched opened the cellar door. It creaked loudly. Without waiting to hear if anybody would come running to investigate, she moved forward onto the top of the cellar steps, closed the door behind her and was immediately swallowed by darkness.

Feeling for every step, she edged her way down. At the bottom it was slow-going, but she didn't dare put on the light. She crept forward, running her hand over the crumbling surface of the wall until she found the opening of the tunnel to the ice house. A damp, musty smell rose as her fingers traced the curve.

The tunnel seemed much longer than she remembered but, at last, her hand touched a smooth, hard, flat surface in front of her. Raking along what she hoped was the top ledge of the door, she touched something cold; it moved, and her hand closed round a key.

The lock was stiff and took precious minutes to open. Maya cursed softly as she snagged a nail and hurt her bandaged hand, but eventually she succeeded – the key turned. Wedging her shoulder against the door, she gave a few mighty pushes and shot out like a cannonball into the garden and daylight.

Blinking as sunlight flooded her eyes, she looked around – thankfully the coast was clear, there were no police or agents lurking about. But it wasn't only cops that worried her; Simon had warned her, 'Be vigilant, keep close to the house, these fanatics will stop at nothing.'

Anxious to disappear as quickly as possible, she sprinted over the grass, dodging into the nearest bush. Ducking low, she made her way under the trees towards the stile, leapt over it in one fast fluid movement and was onto the woodland path. It was tempting to look back to see if anyone was following, but she resisted. Instead, she adjusted the straps of her rucksack and started to run.

Eyes gleamed from the shadows, twigs cracked, leaves rustled. If anyone was watching, Maya knew she was an open target. The only thing she could do was run fast, retracing her footsteps from this morning, dodging under low branches, sliding down the bank, leaping the stream. The marathon training paid off – even with the heavy bag on her back, she flew. Everything blurred into ripples of green and brown, and then she was aware only of the sun dancing on her face, the sweat prickling her back, the rhythm of her feet and the need to get to the railway station.

At the top of the wood she climbed the stile into an open field. If she could make it through there, then she thought she'd be OK. Glancing over her shoulder, she started to run downhill to the dark ribbon of road. Cars flashed along the valley floor, the sun rippled over the long grass. She was beginning to feel safe, when suddenly a helicopter rose from the hill behind her, the throbbing engine swamping her ears.

Convinced it had been sent to search for her, Maya looked desperately for cover. There was nothing – not even a tree or bush. She shielded her eyes. It was coming closer, sun glinting on the round, perspex bulge of the cockpit, any moment she'd be spotted. Then, out of the corner of her eye, she saw a horse. Without much hope she pulled her bag from her back, dropped it on the ground and whistled.

Come on. Please believe I've got a nice treat for you in my pocket.

She whistled again and the horse lifted its head, turned and came galloping, full pelt.

Over her shoulder the helicopter was getting closer; soon the pilot would be able to see her face. But with a small earthquake the horse ground to a halt and stood in front of her. She put an arm round its neck, felt in her pocket and – glory of glories! – she found half a packet of polo mints. The horse smelt them and Maya hid her face in its thick mane as the helicopter flew overhead.

As the horse was nuzzling for the last polo mint, the helicopter disappeared from sight, and it didn't return until Maya had skipped down the hill and was crossing the river bridge in front of the railway station. If the crew had been sent to spot her, they hadn't succeeded.

In the station she bought a ticket for Leeds and waited for an anxious twenty minutes on the platform. At any moment she expected a shadow to fall across her, a hand to grab her shoulder, but nobody approached and when the train arrived she knew she was going to make it. She'd escaped, and now she could put her plan into action.

* * *

While the train rumbled along, Maya tried to work out what she was going to do. She had to admit her plan wasn't exactly watertight, but she was certain that all the evidence pointed to the Leeds group. If she could get to talk to Khaled Husain, she'd make him give her information and she would get it quicker than Simon's team could. She'd find her mum, and together they'd stop the bombs. Even if she was wrong or her plan was crazy, she had to try. And if Khaled Husain was the one who'd betrayed Pam – a double agent? It was a chance she had to take.

The train journey seemed to take forever. She wished she could contact Simon and ask him what was happening at the farmhouse. If only he had agreed to use her to suss out the bookshop, then she would have backup.

The train jolted and stopped suddenly, panicking her. This was ridiculous, she had to control her nerves; only if she was calm could she think clearly. Looking out of the window, she saw the train was standing at a little country station, and for a moment she was tempted to get off, turn round and run back home.

Doubts plagued her mind, nibbling at her brain like maggots. What if Pam had phoned home with another message? What if she'd already been rescued? But even if this had happened, Maya knew she had to carry on; she had to find Khaled and get the all-important information her mum needed.

She rested her elbows on the table in front of her as the train started up again. The plants and bushes outside blurred into swathes of green and yellow. Simon could play his waiting game, ask his team to keep watch and gather intelligence, but Maya was certain that Pam's kidnapping was connected to the Leeds cell. And if Khaled knew where Pam was being held, if he had a clue about the hiding-place, somehow she'd make him tell her.

It wouldn't be easy. She'd have to be alert, cautious, scope Khaled out before she revealed who she was. Could she present herself as a Muslim girl? She had tried to forget everything about her religion – now she tried desperately to remember. Maybe the sensible thing to do was to say she was on a quest to learn.

As the train pulled into Leeds City station, she was full of trepidation. She'd never been to Leeds before, had only a vague idea of where she wanted to go, and knew it was quite possible that police would be on the platform waiting for her.

Occupying the seat opposite her, long legs sprawled under the table, was a gum-chewing lad wearing a baseball cap. He'd been a bit of a pain, to be honest – taking up most of the leg room, a copy of *The Sun* spread out over the table, elbows planted – but the baseball cap he was wearing gave

Maya an idea.

'Cool cap,' she said to him.

He looked at her as if she were mad.

She smiled at him. 'Give you a tenner for it.'

Now he knew she was mad.

'Cost me more than that,' he shot back.

'But it's not new, is it?'

He took if off and looked at it. 'Nah. 'He stared at her. 'What do ya want it for?'

'My boyfriend's meeting me. I haven't seen him for six months. I want to see if he recognises me with that cap on.'

His face wrinkled. 'Ten quid for a bit of a joke. You rich or somethin'?'

She shrugged.

He eyed her to see if the offer was still on. Maya gave him a nod.

'OK,' he said. 'Done.'

He shoved the cap across the table and Maya reached for her purse.

'Are you from Leeds?' she asked him.

'Yeah.'

'Do you know where Hyde Park is?'

'Yeah.'

'How do I get there?'

'Number ninety-six bus.'

'Thanks.'

He took her money. The train was stopping. He stood up and watched her put on the cap. 'You wanna stick all your hair under it,' he said. Then he gave her a hard stare. 'You'll still look like a Paki, though, won't you?'

Chapter Nine

The number ninety-six double-decker shuddered past shabby shop fronts, graffitied walls and blowing litter. On board, the atmosphere was cheerful, with passengers exchanging loud greetings. It was a mixed bunch; in front of Maya a black guy in a Leeds football shirt was chatting to his grandson; over the aisle a group of women in bright dresses were speaking their own language, and when the bus stopped two women in full black robes and veils got on and walked past her. She didn't feel out of place. The lad on the train who'd called her 'Paki' had given her confidence – she reckoned she blended in.

Where to get off the bus was a problem, but when it passed a green-domed mosque and shops with Arabic writing above the windows, it didn't take much brainpower to work out that this would be a good place to start her search. The bus slowed down and a group of five women dressed in dark clothing got up. Maya followed them. The women stood on the pavement talking, while Maya pretended to study the jewelled fruits on display at the Begum Fruit Emporium. When their chatter faded and it seemed as if they were going their separate ways, Maya plucked up courage and stepped forward.

'Excuse me. Could you tell me how to get to the Red Moon bookshop?'

Five pairs of eyes stared at her. A woman with a wide, smooth forehead under a white headscarf said something in her own language to her friend. Her friend replied without taking her eyes off Maya. It was unnerving. Perhaps they didn't understand her, and if they did, they'd probably never heard of the bookshop – most likely she was in the wrong area altogether. She was debating whether to walk away when one of the older women, her grey hair uncovered, turned to her.

'Why are you wanting the bookshop?'

'I . . . I . . . need some information,' Maya said.

'What about? Her voice was so sharp and direct that Maya almost walked off, but just in time she remembered the lines she'd rehearsed on the train.

'I'm a student,' she said. 'I'm writing a dissertation about the politicisation of young Muslims. I was told the Red Moon bookshop has lots of up-to-date stuff.'

The woman's harsh hawk-like face suddenly split into a smile. 'The bookshop is very good,' she said. 'My nephew Khaled will help you.'

Maya couldn't believe it. She'd hit the jackpot first time. She stood amazed, as the the grey-haired woman gave her directions.

'Cross over the road, go past the clinic and turn right. You will see the bookshop in front of you.'

'Thank you,' Maya replied.

As she walked away she was followed by ripples of laughter. She didn't know what they were finding so amusing, but at least they seemed friendly and for that she was grateful. She was trying not to think about what might be happening to her mum, but images haunted her like bad dreams – she saw her tied up and gagged, her face marked with bruises, her eyes dulled with pain. Instantly she pushed the pictures to the back of her mind – but the clock was ticking.

* * *

It was Pam's lowest moment. She rubbed the side of her face where the man had hit her with the phone. He'd been angry because she'd added the message to Maya about the moon. Afterwards she'd tried to convince him that it was a custom she and Maya followed when they were apart – each of them looking at the moon and thinking about the other. She could see that the woman half-believed her, but the man was suspicious.

'You know what we agreed,' the man said.

Pam wasn't sure she'd agreed to anything, but she knew she didn't want them to hurt Maya.

'I'm sorry,' Pam said. 'I knew my daughter was upset so I wanted to comfort her.'

'Your daughter will be beyond comfort if you disregard our orders,' the man said angrily. 'Omar will not be pleased.'

Pam rubbed at her bruised cheek. 'Then why do you need to tell him?' she said softly.

The man scoffed and spat on the floor. 'We Muslims are not double-dealers and liars like you kafirs. Omar must be told. He must be warned. The girl could cause him trouble.'

* * *

The Red Moon bookshop was at the top of a side street that led off the main road. From across the street, the crimson shop front decorated with gold crescent moons looked like a store that might sell children's toys. As Maya stood checking out the premises she saw a dark figure slip away from an adjacent doorway and melt into the shadow of the buildings. Crossing the road she felt exposed, her skin prickled – somebody was watching her – but if it was one of the surveillance team, they didn't challenge her.

The door of the bookshop creaked and jangled as she tentatively stepped inside to look around. Shafts of sunlight striped the tall bookshelves, lighting up golden Arabic lettering on thick, leather-bound volumes. Paperbacks with titles such as *One Faith* and *Islam in the Modern World* were on display. There seemed to be nobody about, no owner or customer, but even so, her heart was racing – she felt as if she'd crossed enemy lines.

Nervously she edged towards the counter, took off the cap and bent to look at some pamphlets.

'Can I help you?'

The words vibrated softly in the dusty room. She turned, but couldn't see anyone. Then, soft as a shadow, he appeared from behind a bookcase and without a sound he was standing in front of her; the man with the green eyes, his photograph come to life. Maya was totally dumbfounded.

'I . . . I . . . er . . . I came . . . I came to buy a book.'

'Well, you've come to the right place.'

His voice was surprisingly deep and mellow. His eyes rippled with translucent light: they were the most beautiful eyes she'd ever seen. Captivated, all she could do was stare.

'I'm Khaled,' he said.

She had to look away to gather her thoughts. 'I was told you'd be able to help me,' she said. 'I need some information.'

'Yes, what about?'

She dared herself to look at him again; his eyes held hers. Her thoughts broke into pieces, her words stumbled out. 'I'm a student,' she managed to say, 'writing a special study.'

'Yes, what is your subject?'

'Erm, Muslim youth,' she replied. 'Why young Muslims are disenchanted with British society.'

His eyebrows arched; he looked slightly amused. 'Perhaps not all young Muslims,' he said.

She gulped, studied a poster on the wall, her mouth

dry, her nerves dancing. He stepped closer. 'Don't believe everything you read in the newspapers.'

The way he was looking at her made her nervous.

'Are you Muslim?' he asked.

A shiver of panic ran through her. She forced herself to concentrate, to remember her story; she had to hide her identity until she knew for certain whose side he was on.

'I was adopted by an English family,' she told him, 'a Christian family, but my birth family was Muslim.'

'So, is that the real reason you're here?' he asked.

Again those searching eyes. She caught her breath and swallowed. Her voice came out in a low croak.

'I . . . I had. . .' She coughed to clear her throat, then tried again. 'I had a row with my parents, my . . . my adopted parents, they . . . er . . . they don't understand me needing to find out about my background, to trace my roots.'

He nodded slowly, processing the information, then he relaxed. 'Allah is calling you,' he said. 'Praise be His name. You have left your family to find the truth.' He gestured to the back of the shop. 'Come with me.'

Chapter Ten

Maya watched nervously as Khaled went over to the shop door, locked it and flipped the OPEN sign to CLOSED. Then she followed him out of the shop into a dark stairwell.

'Wait,' he said.

She stood hovering near the door, uncertain what he intended, not knowing if she could trust him. He darted forward and flicked on a light. A bare bulb illuminated a small kitchen. The work surfaces and paintwork were old and chipped but it was spotlessly clean. On a scrubbed table gleamed several sharp-bladed knives.

'Come on in,' he said.

Checking for exits, Maya stepped into the room. There was a back door, but as far as she could tell it led into a small enclosed yard. The only way out was the way she'd come in. She glanced over her shoulder, wondering if she should escape while it was still possible.

'Sit down,' he said.

She gave one last backward glance into the bookshop, then slowly moved towards him. He pulled out a chair. She hesitated, her eyes catching the glint of knife blades splayed across the table – a small, lethal-looking dagger, a long bread knife, a heavy meat cleaver.

A gentle smile played around Khaled's lips as he stood resting his hands on the back of her chair. 'Put your bag down. Make yourself at home.'

Obediently Maya dropped her bag and sat down, aware that his hands were only a few centimeters from her shoulders. She tensed, and gritted her teeth as he leaned over her. Her eyes half-closed; she was almost greedy for his touch, imagined his fingers snaking round her throat. Would she fight, or would she just give in? Why the hell hadn't she thought to get Mum's gun, taken it from the safe in the house?

She licked her lips and swallowed, her eyes darted to the table. Almost within reach was the handle of a small, pointed knife, if she edged forward she could grab it and strike. Her hand twitched as Khaled's weight rocked the chair, she sensed the warmth of him, smelt a hint of lemony cologne or aftershave. Silence buzzed, seconds ticked by and Maya's heart went into overdrive. Why was he so still? What was he planning?

Eventually she could stand it no longer. Screwing up her courage, she tilted back her head and dared to look up at him. His skin was a smooth, hazelnut brown curving over fine cheekbones, a curl of dark silky hair fell over one ear. He appeared to be deep in thought.

When he caught her looking up at him, he blinked. From under his long, dark lashes his eyes hooked onto hers. Maya held her breath, and then suddenly he was gone.

'Would you like a cup of tea?'

Maya breathed out a long sigh of relief.

Khaled stood with his back against the sink, one long, slender arm supporting his weight. 'There's not much custom today. Doesn't matter if I close early.' He stretched out a hand reaching for the kettle. 'You're not from round here, are you? Where do you live?'

'Derbyshire,' Maya said, weakly, thinking too late that she should have lied.

'So, are you staying with relatives?'

'No. I just came up today to try and find some information.'

He raised one delicate eyebrow. 'Why here? Why Leeds?'

'I . . . I . . . just knew it was where a lot of Muslims lived.'

'So, why not Derby? A lot of Muslims live there too.'

She bit her lip, gulped, then, casting her eyes downward, she said quietly, 'I just wanted to get away.'

'I understand.'

The kettle boiled and he turned to make tea and put some biscuits onto a plate. She noted his elegant hands, his delicate movements, his tall, slim body, and reminded herself that he was Khaled Husain, the man with green eyes – the man with an asterisk under his photo that marked him as a suicide bomber. Was he somebody prepared to kill and die for his faith? If he knew who she was, would he help her or betray her?

He put two mugs on the table. 'Do you

take sugar?'

'No thank you.'

She drew the mug towards her. He sat down, leaned across the table and asked abruptly, 'How did you manage to find this place?'

'I got off the bus and asked where there was a good bookshop. A grey-haired woman who said she was your aunt directed me here.'

He looked away, then back. 'Hm. That would be Mariam,' he said. He sipped his tea, his eyes glimmering over the rim of the white mug. 'A bookshop,' he said, with a wry smile. 'Out of the whole of England, you found this one.'

'I thought an Islamic bookshop would be a good place to start learning about Islam,' Maya shot back at him.

'What's your name?'

'Soraya,' she replied without hesitation, giving the name of a Muslim girl in her class at school.

He looked thoughtful. 'So, Soraya, are you willing to give your life to Allah, to follow the teachings of our Prophet, peace be upon him?'

She drew back her shoulders and held her head high. 'I want to learn, to grow, to make an informed decision. It's my birthright.' The words surprised her, she had no idea where they came from.

Khaled cupped his chin with his thumb and forefinger and said, with a half-smile, 'You've been denied the truth for too long.'

His stare was intense, his eyes mesmerising, and Maya found she couldn't look away. She sipped her tea and blinked, but his gaze was still there, examining, assessing, making her hand shake as she set down her mug. He leaned forward, looked as if he was going to say something, then abruptly changed his mind, got up and went over to a shelf, where he picked out a small slim book.

'Here,' he said. 'This is a good place to start.'

He came over and handed the book to her. She looked at the title – *The Five Pillars of Islam*.

'You're welcome to join one of our study groups.'

'Thank you. That'd be great, but I don't have anywhere to stay.'

'You can stay here. I'll show you where, when you've drunk your tea. See what you think.'

Maya was eager to look round the place, but not with Khaled watching her every move.

'Is there a toilet?' she asked.

'Yes, of course. Up the stairs, first door on

your right.'

On the staircase were big posters printed with Arabic script; one had the graphic image of a bloodstained dagger plunged into a map of the Middle East, and another showed George Bush's face behind barbed wire. Maya opened and closed the bathroom door, remaining on the outside.

Tiptoeing along the corridor, she pushed open the door to the next room, checked there was nobody inside and walked in. Picking her way carefully over bedding and a heap of prayer mats, she went over to a long table. A pile of pamphlets with the word JIHAD in bold lettering attracted her attention. She knew that jihad was about fighting a holy war for Allah. She opened the pamphlet and read the headline – ISRAEL IS AN ILLEGAL STATE.

At the other side of the table was an article torn out of a newspaper about a plot to bomb Britain and beside it was another pile of leaflets that had the heading, BRITISH VALUES??? The leaflet showed cartoons of teenagers – football yobs causing trouble, scantily-dressed girls dancing, and what she assumed were victims of drug-taking and drunkenness lying in doorways and vomiting in gutters. *Is this what we want for our youth?*

the article asked.

Moving back from the table, she glanced around. The sound of a door opening downstairs sent her running back to the bathroom and she slipped inside and flushed the loo. When she came out, she heard the kitchen door open below her and Khaled came running up the stairs holding her rucksack.

'Here,' he said, 'you should keep this with you.'

His fingers touched hers as she grasped the handle of the bag; just the slightest, gentlest brush of skin, but she found it unnerving. He was mysterious: aloof yet friendly, suspicious but hospitable. She couldn't work him out. She was considering the evidence, when she saw that the straps of her rucksack were undone and flapping.

He ignored her questioning look. 'Come on, I'll show you round,' he said, leading the way back into the room she'd just visited.

'Who stays here?' she asked.

'Followers.'

'Oh.'

'You'll see. It's another world in here, a completely different world.'

'OK, but. . .'

He interrupted. 'You're thinking it's not right for

a young woman to be amongst men. Don't worry, Lubna will be here soon. She organises the women. She'll take care of you.'

'Does everybody sleep in here?' she asked.

'No. There's another room for the women.'

She looked away, feeling embarrassed. There was a noise on the stairs, and a young woman wearing jeans and a headscarf entered.

'Here's Lubna,' Khaled said. 'Lubna, this is Soraya. She's going to be staying with us for a while.'

Lubna wasn't pretty. Her forehead under the pale blue silk scarf was broad and moles of various sizes sprinkled her round cheeks, but her smile lit up her face. Maya tried to remember if she'd seen her photo on the computer, but she couldn't honestly be sure.

'Hello. Good to meet you,' Lubna said.

Khaled became a bit more detached, businesslike. 'Look after her, will you?' he asked Lubna.

Lubna lowered her eyes. 'Yes, of course.' Then she looked up at him. 'Are you going to speak at the meeting?'

'Yes.'

They exchanged knowing looks and Lubna smiled at him. 'Peace be upon the servant of Allah for the manifold blessings he showers upon us each day. Allah be praised.'

'Allah be praised,' Khaled said quietly. Then he added, 'We must be on our guard, Lubna. There are some who don't want peace – peace makes enemies.'

His eyes rested on Maya. A wave of heat prickled her neck and face. Were his words aimed at her? Had he looked in her bag? Did he know her real identity? Was the game up?

Chapter Eleven

A silver Mercedes drove through the big iron gates of a large house and came to rest on the back drive. The car door opened, and out stepped a bearded man in a shiny suit. He reached for a briefcase, locked the car door and went into the kitchen of his home.

His wife, Shameen, met him with a worried face. She was holding a big pile of laundry.

'Omar, we'll never be ready in time. Why do we have to go so soon? There's so much to do. I haven't packed Jasmina's clothes yet. She wants to take so much. Can't we delay our flight for a couple of days?'

Omar bent to remove his shoes. 'These need to be cleaned,' he said, holding them out to his wife.

His wife dumped the laundry on the worktop. 'I have so much to do,' she moaned, as she took the shoes into the utility room.

Omar took off his suit jacket, put on a pair of leather slippers and scratched his ample stomach. 'I told you,' he shouted to his wife, 'I got a good deal on the tickets. Transporting six people to Lahore is not cheap.'

His wife came back into the room and started to bring up another complaint, but he waved her away. 'Get the girls to help you. I'm tired. I've been driving all day.'

Shameen backed away, her eyes averted. 'Sit down. I'll get you something to eat and drink.' She moved the laundry on to a chair. 'Did you meet the suppliers?' she asked.

'What?' Omar said, busy emptying his pockets onto the table.

'The suppliers you went to see in Derby?'

'Oh, er . . . yes.'

'And was it a successful trip?'

'Yes, very.'

'I have to ask you something,' his wife said as she opened the fridge door.

'What?'

'Jamila doesn't want to go with us. She has studying to do. She's taking her A levels next year, you know.'

Omar sat at the table and thumped his fist down hard. 'Jamila cannot make her own decisions.'

'She wants to stay here with her grandfather.'

Omar cut in loudly, 'I can't be bothered with this. I have important business to attend to. Jamila will go with you. It's bad enough that my father refuses to go.'

'He's too old to make such a long journey,' his wife said quietly.

'Nonsense. The family would like to see the great Professor Sharif. They all remember him with great affection. And his brilliant son Majid, of course. What a pity they don't honour the great Omar, the one who sends the money that feeds them all.'

'Of course they honour you,' his wife said. 'They'll be glad to see us. We'll provide fine wives for their sons.'

'Yes, while you're there you can find a suitable husband for Jamila. I've had enough of this studying nonsense.'

'She would like to be a doctor,' his wife said softly.

Omar snorted. 'She doesn't need a career. Her husband will provide.' His eyes flew to the door as his father came in.

'What are you shouting about now?' Sharif asked.

'He wants Jamila to go with us to Pakistan,' Shameen explained.

'She's staying with me,' his father said.

Omar looked as if he was going to protest, then he said sulkily, 'Is a man not the boss in his own house?'

His wife put a plate of rice and mutton on the table. 'Here, please eat. You'll feel better.'

Omar stood up. 'No. Save it. I have no time to eat now. I must prepare for an important meeting.'

'But you've only just come home,' Shameen protested.

'I'm going into the study,' Omar said sharply, snatching up a handful of food.

Before he could walk out, his father, Sharif, stopped in front of him. 'These meetings are the root cause of our troubles,' he said. 'Because of you, your brother is detained in prison. Do not set something in motion that you cannot stop.'

'I know what I'm doing,' Omar snapped.

His father raised his eyebrows. 'It would be for the first time,' he said.

Omar's chin wobbled, his bottom lip protruded and his whole body seemed to bristle and shake as he bustled past his father, down the hallway and into his study.

He opened the door onto a richly furnished room. An oak desk stood in the middle of the floor on a silk rug. Behind the desk were a padded leather chair and substantial bookcases. It was the study of an important man.

Omar was setting down his expensive briefcase when the phone rang.

'Yes?'

He listened for a moment, then said, 'Ah yes, the daughter.'

There was another brief silence, during which he sat down.

'Put out the word,' he said, leaning back in his chair. 'This time there will be no mercy.'

* * *

'Come with me,' Lubna said. 'I'll show you where to put your things.' She bowed her head solemnly as they left the room but outside she gave Maya a friendly smile.

'What brought you here?' she asked.

'A quest.'

'For faith?'

'Yes.'

Lubna's eyes lit up. 'If you find the enlightened path, the way of Allah and His prophet Muhammad, praise be his name, you will find truth, you will find peace.'

'That's what I'm looking for,' Maya said. 'Some kind of certainty in a crazy world.'

Lubna put her hand over her heart. 'I know what you mean. My faith is the most important thing in my life. I couldn't live without it – it's my rock, it shows me how to live.'

'Do you ever question it?' Maya asked.

'No. It's a part of me. Without my faith, my life would have no meaning. For Muslims, when we submit to God, we obey His laws. Everything is God's will and we are a part of His eternal plan; nothing is random. So this gives me certainty and peace.'

'That's wonderful,' Maya said.

Lubna clasped her hands. 'Yes, it is. There are so

many bad things going on, so much crime, drugs, so much disrespecting of women.'

'But I thought—' The words were out of Maya's mouth before she could stop them.

'You thought Muslim women were not respected? You think we're second-class citizens.'

'Well, I . . . I suppose, you know, you read in the newspapers about the Taliban, about women not being able to drive cars or have careers, having to be covered up, being stoned to death.'

'We women accept our fate. We learn humility but we are respected by our men. A Muslim woman has full rights of property ownership and her own earnings even after marriage, and she keeps her own family name. Is that a surprise to you?'

Maya nodded, she had to admit it was.

'And this,' Lubna said, indicating her headscarf. 'I don't have to cover my head. I do it because of tradition, but also because I want to acknowledge my faith in public. I want people to know I'm Muslim.'

'But doesn't it feel restricting?'

'No. For me it's natural. Come on, I'll show you.'

She took Maya into a room at the back of the shop. It was smaller than the other room, but much brighter. There was a big sofa covered with an orange throw, a little table with a jar of sunflowers on it and some vivid paintings on the walls. Opening a drawer in a cabinet she pulled out a white headscarf, her face became serious. 'I'll show you how to wear the hijab.'

The white material fluttered in front of Maya's face. Lubna demonstrated how to fold it, then pulled it tight across Maya's forehead and secured it with clips.

'Thank you,' Maya murmured.

'Here,' Lubna said, handing her a small mirror.

Maya looked at her reflection and saw a Muslim girl – perfectly smooth arched eyebrows, high cheekbones and tawny skin. Her brown almond eyes looked back at her, dark and disturbed.

'You're beautiful,' Lubna said, taking the mirror.

Opening another drawer, she took out some perfume. 'Do you like Chanel?'

'Yes,' said Maya, surprised.

'Good.' Lubna removed the cap and sprayed some perfume on Maya's scarf and then on her own. Laughing, she turned round and closed the cabinet drawer. 'The finishing touch,' she said.

'Do you have a radio or TV here?' Maya asked.

'Why?'

'I just wondered.'

'We have no need of such things here. We study.'

'What about Khaled? Is he in charge?

'He's one of the teachers.' She fiddled with her headscarf, blushed and looked away.

'Is he a devout Muslim?' Maya asked.

'Of course.'

Lubna's sharp response made Maya feel she'd asked the wrong question. To try and win back Lubna's approval, she shared the story she'd made up.

'I was adopted when I was a baby,' she told her. 'My adoptive parents are really nice and they've been good to me. They had to go through a lot of red tape to get me, so I should be grateful. But I've always felt something's missing from life. My real family was Muslim.'

Lubna reached out and put her hands on Maya's shoulders. 'You will be my sister. I will show you our ways.'

'Thank you,' Maya said, smiling warmly.

'You'll have to study,' Lubna said. 'Knowledge is one of the important ideals of Islam. We must respect learning. I'm studying Law at university.'

'Really? That's great,' Maya said. 'Where do

you go?'

'Manchester. The first year was difficult, getting to know people. Most of university social life revolves around pubs and drinking and, as you know, Muslims don't drink alcohol. But now I'm into my third year, I'm enjoying it.'

'That's good,' Maya said.

'When I finish,' Lubna said, 'I want to be a barrister, then marry and have a family.'

'Will your family find you a husband?'

Lubna laughed. 'I think they already have someone in mind.'

'And if you don't like him?'

'My family will choose wisely,' Lubna said. 'But I won't have to marry him if I don't like him. I know it's probably an alien concept to you, but ask yourself what is better – romantic passion that dies after a few years, or a lasting marriage based on respect and family honour?'

Maya's brow wrinkled as she thought about what Lubna had said.

Lubna smiled. 'OK. Read your book while I go and get something for us to eat.'

When she'd gone, Maya looked at the book and tried to concentrate, but her thoughts were dominated by wondering what was happening to her mum and if there'd been any news. Desperate to check her mobile for messages, she made sure nobody was around and then reached into the zip compartment of her rucksack. Her phone wasn't there. She unzipped her bag and searched everything, getting more and more frantic. Finally, when she'd shaken out every item in her bag and piled it all on the floor, she knew for definite her phone had gone. Her mind tracked back – had the lad on the train stolen it? No, she remembered checking her messages later on the bus.

Khaled! He was the only one who could have taken it, and her bag had been open when he'd handed it back to her. She prowled round the room wondering what to do. Had he taken the mobile to check who she was?

As she tried to figure things out, she went over to the window and stared into the little yard below that backed onto a high brick wall. Someone came into view. It was Khaled, and he was carrying something, holding it carefully – it looked like a plate of food, but she couldn't see clearly because outside the window was streaked with grime. She watched his blurred figure as he bent down and pulled at a low door. He disappeared down some steps, closing the door behind him.

All Maya's senses were alert. She had to find out what Khaled was up to. Who was down there, who was he taking food to? Striding over to the door, she looked out onto the landing. Nobody was around, so she stepped out and tiptoed downstairs. Lubna wasn't in the kitchen, it was empty, but the back door had been left slightly open and she went out into the yard.

The small red door was in the high brick wall on the opposite side of the yard. Glancing back over her shoulder, Maya dashed to the door, bent down and pulled at the handle – it wouldn't shift. She tried again without success, then started jiggling the handle, but suddenly the door flew open in her face and she just managed to save herself from falling as she was catapulted backwards.

'Did you want something?'

Khaled was standing there. He stepped forward, his tall figure looming over her, his eyes glittering.

'I . . . er . . . I came out into the yard to . . . to . . . phone my parents and I saw this little door.'

His face creased with annoyance. 'I would prefer it if you would keep to your quarters inside the bookshop.'

'Yes, of course.' she said, but couldn't help adding, 'Why?'

He pressed his lips together and mumbled something about valuable books being stored down there.

Then he put his hand in his pocket and thrust her mobile at her. 'Here, if you want to phone your parents, you'd better have this.'

Maya eyed him with suspicion.

'You left it on the kitchen table,' he said.

She seriously doubted it – she'd never used her phone in the kitchen – but she thought it best not to question him.

'Come on, let's go inside,' he said. 'I have to get ready for a meeting tonight.'

'Can I attend the meeting?' she asked, as she followed him back into the kitchen.

'It's not an open meeting.' He flexed his fingers and cracked a knuckle. 'You must be more careful with that mobile. It could fall into the wrong hands.' He gave her a direct, challenging stare before turning away.

Maya's heart thumped, her stomach tightened. What incriminating evidence had he seen on her mobile? She held her phone tightly in one hand and tapped into the inbox. All her messages had been deleted.

Chapter Twelve

'Did you delete my messages?' Maya snapped.

'If someone else had searched your bag, you'd be in trouble,' Khaled answered.

She faced him squarely, her voice shrill. 'What do you know? Tell me!'

He stepped towards her, his eyes flashing angrily. 'I know who you are, and it's too dangerous for you to be here. You shouldn't have come.'

'Where's my mother?'

'I don't know, I. . .'

From the direction of the shop there was a distinct click, as if someone was shutting a door. Khaled glanced round nervously. 'Leave now!'

'No! I have to find out who's got my mum. Where is she?'

Khaled gestured for calm and spoke softly. 'Please, I'll help you but. . .'

The door to the bookshop opened and closed. Khaled leaned close and whispered urgently. 'You are my cousin, understand?'

Footsteps rapped through the bookshop and a figure appeared in the doorway; a young guy, small and stocky in black jeans and hooded top stepped into view.

Maya caught her breath; he was dressed like the kidnappers. Cold fear gripped her as his eyes swept over her, their gaze dark and intense. Such a burning energy emanated from him that she felt at any moment, he might explode into action. Then she saw something that almost stopped her heart – dangling from his hand was a black hood. A small, involuntary cry came from her throat, she nearly gave herself away but, luckily, at that moment Khaled spoke.

'Nazim, my man,' he said stepping forward. 'How's it going?'

Nazim smiled, showing a wide gap between his top teeth. 'Success, man, success. We caught the rabbit.'

He smirked and chuckled, while Khaled shook his hand.

'Excellent,' Khaled said. 'Did it all go to plan?'

'Yeah, the decoy worked. The hounds are hunting south.'

Khaled nodded and smiled, then he gestured toward Maya. 'Nazim, this is Soraya, she's just joined us.'

Nazim pursed his lips and looked at Maya through narrowed eyes. 'You know her?' he asked Khaled.

Khaled nodded. 'Yeah, I can vouch for her. Soraya's my cousin.'

Nazim rocked back on his heels. 'Right,' he said, 'Cousin. Yeah, OK. Good to meet ya.'

Maya clenched her teeth and cast her eyes down, forcing herself to stay in control. Anger was pricking her tongue, her eyes were riveted to the black hood in his hand. When she looked up, he'd pushed back his hood and she saw the silver scar running across his forehead. She wanted to scream at him, ask him if he knew where her mum was, but that would be suicide.

Her stomach started to churn, her breathing quickened. Would he recognise her? He'd only caught a quick glimpse of her on the lane before he zoomed off in the jeep, and he'd seen her in running gear with her hair in a ponytail – he certainly wouldn't expect to see her with her head covered in the bookshop. If she was careful, very careful, remembered she was Soraya, remembered she was there to learn about Islam, looked suitably humble and hid the anger in her eyes, she might not be discovered.

Behind her, the door banged back and Lubna came in carrying a large, heavy covered tray.

'What's that?' Nazim demanded.

'Culinary delights, courtesy of Omar,' Lubna said, setting the tray on the table.

Omar! Maya remembered the text on her mum's computer – *Omar, self-styled leader of the Allied Brotherhood.*

Nazim rubbed his hands together. 'Good. I'm starving,' he said.

'Is there enough for my cousin Soraya?' Khaled asked Lubna.

'Cousin?' Lubna said, looking surprised.

'Oh, sorry, didn't I tell you? Soraya's my cousin,' Khaled said.

'And we can't have your *cousin* starving, can we?' Nazim chipped in.

Maya didn't like the way he put emphasis on the word 'cousin'; it sounded sarcastic, suspicious.

She looked over at him, but he'd turned his back on her.

Lubna touched Maya's shoulder. 'We have to wash before we eat, Soraya.'

'Oh yes, of course,' Maya answered quickly.

The look of pure hatred on Nazim's face as she passed him spooked Maya. In the bathroom, her hands trembled as she ran them under the tap – she was afraid of him, she couldn't help it. His eyes burned with hate, he'd be capable of anything. But she was angry too. How she'd kept from screaming at him, she didn't know.

Keep calm, Maya, hold it together. Watch him carefully, use all the tricks that Pam taught you. He's not so bright, he's bound to give something away.

And what about Khaled? He'd covered for her, calling her his cousin, but then earlier he'd asked Nazim about the kidnapping – that coded stuff about catching the rabbit hadn't fooled her for a moment. He'd known about the plot to seize Pam, so why hadn't he warned her? Whose side was he actually on?

It was confusing and scary. Without much effort on her part she'd made contact with the Brotherhood, but at any moment it could all blow up in her face.

She felt the touch of Lubna's hand on her arm. 'Soraya. I think your hands are clean enough.'

'Oh.' Maya dropped the soap and turned off the tap. 'Sorry, I was dreaming.'

Lubna smiled and handed her a towel. 'I've got cousins in Derby,' she said.

'Oh, really,' Maya answered, her mind elsewhere. Some more of the code words Nazim had uttered came into her mind. *The decoy worked. The hounds are hunting south.*

With a shiver of excitement she put two and two together. She'd been right, Omar's men wanted the police to think they'd taken Pam to the farmhouse, but they hadn't, they'd brought her north. It made sense. Nazim was here and he was one of the gang. Pam could be close by.

The cellar! Khaled had nearly had a fit when he'd found her at the door. He was warning her away. Her mind raced – she had to get a message to Simon.

Glancing across at Lubna who was waiting patiently, she fished for information. 'It was nice of Omar to send food,' she said. 'Who is he?'

Lubna pressed her lips together. 'Omar's our leader,' she said. 'He's very generous. Soon you will meet him.'

'Is he like a religious leader, then?'

Lubna averted her eyes and opened the bathroom door. 'Remember, the men will eat first,' she said, as she went out onto the landing.

'Lubna,' Maya said, as they were going out of the door.

She hesitated. 'Yes?'

'Did you hear about the kidnapping this morning?'

'Yes, I heard.'

'Do you know anything about it?'

Lubna raised her eyebrows and shrugged. 'Why should I know anything?'

'Because the police think it was done by Muslim extremists.'

A sharp look of anger slashed Lubna's face. 'Who told you that?'

Maya gulped. Before she could think of a convincing answer Lubna stepped forward, her eyes glowing.

'We are faithful to Allah and His prophet Muhammad, peace be upon him. Why is it that in this country, if you believe in something, you're called an extremist?'

'I'm sorry,' Maya said. 'I didn't mean to make you angry.'

Lubna raised her eyebrows and sighed. 'I'm not angry. But you must learn to guard your tongue. People here are sensitive. Come on, or the men will have eaten all the food.'

Maya nodded, eager to get back to the kitchen where she might pick up some useful information.

Khaled and Nazim were sitting at the table. They'd been joined by three other guys and, as Lubna had predicted, they'd eaten most of the food. There were only a few bits of chicken left, but there was rice with vegetables and Lubna served Maya with a heaped bowl.

They sat apart from the men on two chairs by the sink. Lubna settled a book on her lap and was soon absorbed in the text, her lips moving as she read. Maya tried to look as if she was interested in her food and not in their conversation, but her ears were straining.

Nazim was speaking in low but excited tones. 'Omar's coming to the meeting. Now that woman's out of the picture, if he gives the order to go, we'll do it. With Allah's guidance we'll light up the skies, brothers.'

For a moment nobody spoke, but Maya could feel the tension and a palpable sense of excitement. Then Khaled said, 'We don't know how much the woman passed on before she was taken out. What if the Security Forces know all our plans?'

A lad with his back to Maya reared up and scoffed. 'We're not going to let one woman dictate what we can do.'

'They're raiding houses, rounding up brothers. We have to avenge their honour,' another of the boys said. 'It's war.'

'The woman should be sacrificed,' Nazim declared, adding emphasis to his words with a violent throat-cutting gesture.

The bowl of food slipped out of Maya's hand onto her lap, spilling some rice onto her jeans. She looked across at Nazim, sending daggers of hate towards his brain. He turned his head and stared at her. His mouth skewed into a tight, sneering smile, vindictive, nasty, but his eyes showed something else. It was hard to fathom, but she thought it was a glow of triumph.

'Are you all right?' Lubna asked her.

'Yeah, I'm fine,' she managed to say. 'I was up early. I feel a bit light-headed. I need to get some fresh air.'

Khaled got up. 'You'll have to excuse us, we need to get ready for the meeting.'

After the guys had trooped upstairs, Maya opened the kitchen door and stepped outside to reach in her pocket for her phone. Glancing around, she checked the yard was empty, closed the door behind her and then punched in Simon's number.

Her heart raced while she listened to Simon's phone ringing.

Please answer, please.

She held her breath, desperate to hear his voice, but when she did, it was just his voicemail message. After the pips she whispered, 'It's Maya. I'm in Leeds and—'

She stopped abruptly as the door behind her creaked. A small, dark figure stood at her shoulder.

'What you doin' out here?' Nazim asked.

The phone nearly slipped from her hand. 'I . . . I . . . er . . . was just phoning my family.'

'Were you? Don't let me stop you.'

'They . . . er . . . they weren't there. I was just leaving a message.'

'So, finish it.'

'It's OK. I'll do it later.'

'What you doin' here? Who invited you?'

'I'm Khaled's cousin.'

Maya tried to sound offhand, hoping he wouldn't notice how much she was trembling.

'I haven't seen you around here before,' he said.

'No,' she replied. 'I live near Derby.'

'So, why you here now?'

He was watching her closely. One eyebrow rose, the scar on his forehead wrinkled. Ten different answers shot through her head, but she found she couldn't speak.

He chuckled. 'Khaled never told me he had a beautiful cousin in Derby.' He licked his lips and brushed close to her as he moved past. 'Kept that to himself, didn't he? Funny you should arrive today when Omar had business in Derbyshire – important business, momentous.'

While speaking, his eyes examined her face, recording the slightest twitch of a muscle, assessing the meaning of every expression. Panic surged through her as his gaze swept the contours of her face and body. Her throat dried, her nerves sizzled. If he suspected who she was, she was in deep trouble.

She couldn't take her eyes off him as he walked across the yard. Suddenly he turned.

'You'll have to excuse me,' he said, with mock politeness. 'I'm meeting somebody important. They are down there waiting for me. Top secret.'

She caught a glimpse of a twisted smile before he opened the red door and disappeared, closing it firmly behind him.

Glancing back, she saw Lubna at the kitchen window watching her. Her mind racing ahead, she went back into the kitchen and grabbed the bag into which Lubna had put the remains of their meal.

'I'll take this out to the bin,' she said.

'Thank you,' Lubna replied, smiling. 'Then if you come upstairs I'll give you some books and some of our leaflets to study.'

'OK. See you in a minute.'

Outside it was raining lightly now, a strong, musty smell rose from the bin as she opened the lid. She dumped the rubbish inside and then, in a few quick steps, was standing in front of the red door. She bent down and yanked the handle; this time it opened. In front of her was a flight of stone steps leading down to a cellar.

Taking a deep breath, she edged carefully down the stairs. Halfway down, she stopped and listened. She couldn't hear anything.

A few steps from the bottom she paused, and listened again. Her heart was racing, blood thundering in her ears. If somebody came up the stairs she knew she was vulnerable, an easy target – no protection, no weapons. How could she explain what she was doing? But she had to get closer. She had to know who was down there, who Nazim was talking to. She hardly dared admit it, but wasn't there a tiny flaring spark of a possibility that Pam was down there?

That thought drew her onwards. Slowly, quietly she descended into the bare stairwell. Still nothing, no sound. She trod lightly, feeling her way into the darkness, until suddenly a violent spear of light blasted her eyes. She put up her hand to shield her vision, but she couldn't see round or through the dazzling beam.

A cold, steely voice sent a shuddering chill through her. 'Ah, Maya, we've been waiting for you.'

Chapter Thirteen

Maya couldn't see a thing. All she could make out were shadows. Then she was grabbed from behind. She screamed as her arms were pinned to her sides.

She was sure it was Nazim holding her, breathing hot air onto her neck.

'Shut up! It's useless to scream. Nobody can hear you,' he spat.

'Sit her down,' the man in command ordered.

She was jammed into a chair, hands clamped hard onto her shoulders.

'Where's my—' she started to say, but a hand pressed the words back into her mouth.

'Let's get this straight. I ask the questions,' the man in charge said.

She peered into the light, trying to see the

owner of the voice.

'Who are you?' he asked.

'I'm Soraya.'

Fingers dug into her neck, forcing her head back. She could hardly breathe, a horrible gurgling sound came from her throat.

'Let me ask you again. Who are you?'

'I . . . I'm Soraya,' she croaked.

'Why have you come here? Who sent you?'

She couldn't answer. Her tongue was stuck at the back of her throat; she thought she was going to swallow it. In panic, she pushed against the chair, writhing from side to side. Then suddenly she was released, her head lolling forwards. A face loomed in front of her: grey beard, dark hooded eyes. She was sure it was the driver of the silver Mercedes, the man who'd watched as she and Pam ran past him.

'You're too curious, Maya, too curious for your own good,' he said.

'My name's Soraya,' she told him. 'I came to learn how to be a good Muslim.'

The man stooped down until his face was level with Maya's. 'I know who you are,' he said. 'What I want to know is, who sent you?'

His mouth, buried in his grey beard, was soft

131

and pink, it twisted into a half-smile. Maya couldn't stand it. She lunged forward trying to swipe at him. Immediately her arms were grabbed and forced up her back. She yelled out in pain.

The bearded man leant forward and hissed into her face, 'How did you find us?'

'Stop!'

It was Khaled. He was standing somewhere behind her. 'Why are you torturing her?' he asked.

'Do you know who this is?' the man with the beard demanded.

The dazzling light was turned away. She saw Khaled standing in front of her, his white shirt glowing.

'Yes, it's Soraya, my cousin.' He stepped closer and spoke angrily to Maya. 'I told you not to disgrace me. Asking questions all the time. There are some things a woman cannot know.' He grabbed hold of her hand. 'Come with me. You can stay in the women's room and study.'

He turned to the man with the beard. 'I apologise, Omar. Her parents sent her here because she's becoming rebellious. She'll soon learn our ways.'

So it *was* Omar, the leader of the Allied Brotherhood. She could see his sunglasses in his top pocket. He was the crazy driver, the man who'd been watching for her and Pam, waiting for just the right moment to call his army. He was staring at Khaled, his eyes blazing, his white shirt open at the collar, stomach bulging over his black suit trousers, black shoes sparkling. Everyone in the room was silent.

Omar fingered his beard and shook his head. 'She may have fooled you, Khaled,' he said. 'But we know her true identity. This is the daughter of our captive. The woman who tried to ruin all our plans.' He swivelled his head to look at Maya and gave a short, mocking laugh. 'No doubt you have come to find your mother.'

Maya dropped her head and closed her eyes, defeated.

Khaled stepped forward. 'What?' he shouted at her. 'You told me a pack of lies?'

She opened her eyes and glared at him, but said nothing.

He threw back his head and stood tall. 'Omar, I can't believe it. She said she was my cousin Soraya, that her mother sent her to be educated. She's the same age and looks like Soraya, but I admit I haven't seen her for a few years. I can't believe I was such a fool.'

'You have put our organisation at risk,' Omar told him. 'You are either a fool or a traitor. We'll see.'

Omar nodded, and another bearded man in a long grey robe stepped forward and pointed to Maya's jeans pocket.

'Phone,' he said.

Reluctantly Maya handed over her mobile.

'And one more thing,' Omar said. His face came close to hers, she smelt a faint waft of stale sweat. He was no taller than Maya. His dark bushy eyebrows, the wiry hair of his beard, the pink wetness of his mouth filled her vision. He reached down, took her wounded hand, held it up and examined the bandage.

'Oh dear. We must get you a clean one,' he said. Then letting go of one hand, he took the other in a tighter grip, his fingers pinching her ring. 'I need something, a little trinket. Hm. . .This will do.'

Maya tried to snatch her hand away but he held it firmly.

'If you don't give me the ring I'll take something else – a finger, perhaps.'

His soft tone didn't change, but Maya saw that his face was hard as stone. Her fingers stiffened as he pulled off her ruby ring and put it in his pocket.

With an imperious wave of his hand, he snapped out orders. 'Come, leave her,' he said. 'We have more important things to attend to.' Then his tone turned to ice as he spoke to Khaled. 'You stay with me. I'll deal with you after the meeting.'

When they had gone Maya closed her eyes, her fingers touching the place where her ring had been. She rocked and swayed, her mind replaying the last few minutes – padding down the stairs, nervous, hopeful, then that voice hitting her like a slap of cold water, singing out her name.

It had been a trap, Maya realised. Omar had been waiting for her, but how did he know she'd go down to the cellar? Did Khaled betray her? No, he'd tried to save her. She remembered the look Nazim had given her in the yard, his mouth twisted by a cruel smile, a triumphant gleam in his eyes. He knew she'd follow him.

She rubbed at her neck, sore from rough hands; her arms hurt, too, where fingers had dug into her flesh. Anger smouldered in her like a slow fuse until she exploded into action. She dashed across the room, belted up the stairs and pulled at the door. Of course, it was locked. With clenched fists she hammered and yelled. There was no response.

Sadly she turned away and went back down the stairs, then prowled around looking for a way to escape. There were no windows or doors, just blank brick walls. How was she going to get out? Slumping down on the floor, despair came over her like a giant net.

The cold of the concrete floor seeped into her bones and she sat shivering in her thin T-shirt and jacket. What an idiot she'd been to think she could act like a secret agent – she was crazy. But, she asked herself, was it any wonder? What other girls lived with kidnapping threats, had their every movement monitored by security officers, had their mother seized by terrorists? Of course she was crazy, crazy enough to risk everything.

She thought about what Lubna had told her – the Qur'an teaches that nothing is random, everything is God's will.

Well, for the moment she had no choice, she had to accept her fate. All she could do was sit and wait to see what happened. Perhaps Simon would trace her phone message. Perhaps Khaled would sneak in and release her.

She pulled up her knees and hugged herself against the cold. She wouldn't think, she wouldn't allow herself to remember. But the walls began to close in on her, pictures shadowed the dim corners, long-forgotten memories stirred.

It had been dark in that cellar, dark and cold. Day after day she'd had to stay quiet and still. Every time her father left, her mother grew anxious, watching and waiting for him to return. Sometimes there was gunfire, sometimes screams. Her mother would sing softly – a half-remembered song came into her head, words of a language she had tried to forget. And then, with a shock, she remembered her mother's eyes – they were green, the same colour as Khaled's. She couldn't picture the rest of the face – the details were buried, blanked out – her father, her two brothers. She had no recollection of them. For so long she had locked away the past, feeling guilty that she'd survived.

Pressing her lips together she breathed noisily, sucking in and out, refusing to cry. It wasn't the right time to remember. Later, perhaps, when all this was over, but she had to deal with the present – she had to escape. Jumping to her feet, she stretched her limbs and started exploring the room again.

The furniture was jammed together; a table against one wall, chairs at each end, a desk with papers spread upon it. Receipts, bills, the same leaflets she'd seen upstairs and beneath them, a newspaper with a big advertisement circled in red ink.

Omar's Carpet and Antiquities Warehouse
Massive Clearance
Carpets and rugs at Trade Prices
48 Queen's Road
Saturday July 7th

The word CANCELLED had been stamped across the advert.

Underneath the newspaper Maya saw corners of a photograph sticking out. Lifting the paper, her stomach tightened – they were photos of Pam. Some had been copied from newspapers and enlarged, some looked as if they'd been snapped secretly by a surveillance camera – Pam walking into MI5 HQ, Pam driving her car. Then she uncovered a photo of the cottage and one of herself and Pam running through the wood. It was painful. Her mind exploded: she was back on that path, caught in mid-stride, the smell of the wild garlic around her, the warmth of the sun on her face and Pam right next to her.

She shook her head. She had to focus, to stay

in control. There were two possible ways out of the cellar – she'd find a way to open the door, or persuade someone to help her. How long would Omar keep her prisoner? What did he plan to do with her? She tore at her fingernails with her teeth.

Damn! If only she hadn't been so stupid. If she'd let Helen or Simon know what she was doing, then she might have back-up. But she hadn't thought things through. She'd come unprepared and was now a prisoner, just like her mum.

She walked over to the stairwell, her mind a flickering horror film – hostages shot, beheaded. Would it hurt? Would she die instantly? She kicked at the wall. She wouldn't give in to such sick thoughts.

Looking up the stairs she saw the red door at the top. If she could find some sort of tool, then maybe she could work on the lock. Turning round, she went back into the room and over to the desk. She opened all the drawers, but there was nothing in them apart from a few tea bags and rolls of duct tape. In a small pot on top of the desk she found paper clips, and was in the process of straightening one out to see if she could pick the lock, when the outside door rattled and footsteps rapped down the stairs. Her neck went icy cold, she stiffened with fear, but it wasn't Omar or any of his heavies – it was Lubna carrying a tray.

'I've brought you some water,' she whispered.

'I don't want water. I want to get out. Will you help me?' Maya asked.

'Shush!' Lubna warned. 'I'm not even supposed to speak to you.'

Maya's eyes were steely. 'Do you have a key?'

'No. One of Omar's men unlocked the door. He's waiting for me upstairs.'

'You can't leave me down here,' Maya pleaded.

Lubna put a finger to her lips. 'Quiet! They'll hear you.' Setting the tray down on the table, she turned and headed for the stairs.

Maya followed, grabbing at her hand. 'Please Lubna, you don't understand. Omar's got my mum, he'll kill her, he'll kill both of us.'

Lubna glanced anxiously over her shoulder, then drew herself up and said calmly, 'Praise be to Allah, who sees all things and will take care of you.'

Maya clasped her hand. 'Omar's wicked,' she said urgently. 'He's planning to plant bombs, kill thousands of people.'

Lubna tried to shake her off. 'I don't believe you.'

'Ask Khaled. He'll tell you. Why do you think

they captured my mum?'

'I don't know. It's not my place to ask. She must be an enemy.'

'I'll tell you why. It's because my mum knows about the plot. She was trying to stop the bombing.'

Lubna looked panic-stricken. 'Let go,' she said, pushing Maya away. 'Stop this, or they'll come for you.'

'You're just frightened for yourself.'

Lubna stared at Maya, then she took a deep breath. 'I'm not afraid,' she said firmly. 'I must be true to my faith.'

Maya let go of her hand. 'I pity you,' she said. 'You're not free to think for yourself – to know evil.'

Lubna reeled as if she'd been slapped, then took flight up the stairs. Maya watched her go.

When she was about halfway up, she paused and whispered something over her shoulder. It sounded like, 'Peace be with you.'

Chapter Fourteen

Pam rubbed her arms and shoulders. They were stiff and sore from the long journey she'd made, crammed in the boot of a car. It had been horribly bumpy. Her head was aching, her nose still full of noxious fumes. When they'd driven away from the farmhouse she'd tried to follow the route, tracking north, east and west, but eventually she'd given up – there were too many twists and turns and she felt sick.

Before she was taken out of the boot she was blindfolded again, but this time the scarf wasn't tied as tightly, and under the bottom of the material she saw a smooth tarmac yard, the wheel arch of a silver car close by, and then the huge granite base stones of an old building, possibly a factory or a mill. When they marched her forwards she heard some doors rolling back as if they'd arrived at a garage or warehouse. Her arm was held in a firm grip until the doors closed behind her.

'You were told to wait till dark,' an angry voice barked.

The man holding Pam replied, 'They were closing in on us. We had to get her out before we were surrounded.'

'Omar's not here yet. Put her in the room.'

It was a short walk from the big, echoing empty space into a narrow corridor. A door was opened and Pam was pushed inside. She stood uncertainly in the middle of the room. The door was firmly locked behind her and she had a strong feeling that this was where she was meant to be; she'd arrived at her destination, whatever the gang had in mind for her, this was where it would happen. She was filled with dread.

Exhausted, she sank down on the cold floor and tried to keep her mind from despairing. If Simon and his team had fallen for the terrorists' decoy, if they thought she was in the farmhouse, they'd play a waiting game, and that waiting could cost her her life. But if Maya had understood the clue about the moon and passed it on, there was hope.

The door of her cell opened. A soft footstep sounded. A hand touched her hair and untied the blindfold. She got to her knees and looked around.

She was in a small room with bare stone walls. To her right was a camp bed covered with rough grey blankets; on the back wall was a small, high window and underneath it two simple wooden chairs. Looking up, she saw a pretty young woman with dark glowing eyes. A few strands of hair had escaped from under her headscarf, her expression was serious.

'Who are you?' Pam asked her.

'My name is not important. I'm here to look after you.'

'Will you untie my hands? The rope's cutting into my wrists.'

'I have no authority to do that.'

The door opened and a bearded man in a grey, shiny suit entered.

'Sit down, please,' he said, gesturing to a chair.

Pam got to her feet, moved over to the chair and sat down. The man placed a chair in front of her, sitting opposite, his knees nearly touching hers.

'My name is Omar,' he said. 'Perhaps you've heard of me?'

Pam sat erect and gazed directly into his face. She shook her head. 'No, I don't think so.'

He laughed. 'And I think you're lying,' he said. 'A surveillance team has been watching our bookshop for some weeks now. I wonder who sent them. Anyway, no matter. I have some news for you. Your daughter's missing. Police are hunting for her.'

An icy hand gripped Pam's throat, her body went rigid, but she made her face stay blank and expressionless.

The man smiled. 'Ah, so that doesn't concern you? I was wondering why she'd leave such a comfortable country home. I wondered if perhaps she's looking for her mother.'

Pam remained silent, tight-lipped.

'Unfortunately,' he continued, 'I think you gave her an important clue. You told her to look for the moon, which led her to the Red Moon bookshop.'

His hooded eyes were like a hawk's, missing nothing. He saw Pam take in a short gasp of breath, bite her bottom lip, noted the slight tremble of her chin. He sat back on his chair, still smiling, looking relaxed, then he nodded and gave a throaty chuckle. His hand reached into his pocket, he stuck his fist in front of Pam's face, then his fingers opened slowly –

there in his palm was Maya's ring, the ruby sparkling like a jewel of blood.

For a moment Pam was mesmerised, then she cried out and lunged forward, wanting to snatch the ring. But her hands were tied and all she could do was slice at the air as Omar got up and moved away.

Perilously close to tears, Pam squeezed her eyes tight shut, then opened them to glare at Omar. 'What have you done with my daughter?' she demanded.

He sniffed and cleared his throat. 'Don't worry, I have daughters of my own. She'll be well looked after.'

'Please don't hurt her,' Pam breathed.

Omar pouted and his mouth made a little popping sound. 'If you want to see her alive again, you'll do as I say.'

'What? What can I do?' Pam whispered.

'First you'll tell us who's been feeding you information. Then you will issue a statement which we will broadcast. After your colleagues have heard it, I doubt they'll want you back.'

Chapter Fifteen

The night was long. Maya paced the room, went up the stairs and tried the door endlessly. It was always locked.

She thumped the walls, kicked the furniture, called Omar every foul name she could think of, then sat down exhausted and told herself to calm down. No plan would work if her vision was clouded by anger. It was difficult to be calm, though. How long did Omar plan to keep her in the cellar? What was he going to do with her? What had he done with her mum? What were Simon and his team up to? So many questions, and she wanted answers, but most of all she wanted to get out of this horrid, cold cellar.

She had to keep her mind clear – she had to sleep.

Jamming two chairs together to form a makeshift bed, she switched off the light and lay down, but in the darkness the demons came, bloody images flickering through her head, and when she finally fell asleep, it was broken by terrifying dreams.

She woke up shivering, rolled off the chairs and fumbled to switch on the lamp. Light spilled over the desk and onto the photos of Pam. She snatched one up and stared at her mum's face; seeing her so full of life and energy brought back hope.

Hold on, Mum. I'll get out of here. Somehow I'll get out and I'll find you.

She folded the photo carefully and put it inside her jacket pocket.

On the tray Lubna had brought stood a glass of water and a few biscuits. Remembering the tea bags in the drawer, Maya fished one out, poured the glass of water into the electric kettle, let it boil, then poured it back into the glass to make tea.

Warming her hands on the glass, she sat at the desk, her mind assessing her chances of being rescued. If Simon's surveillance team were doing their job properly, wouldn't they wonder what had happened to her? Surely they'd be searching for her. If she was in this cellar much longer, she'd go crazy. There was no place to wash, no toilet, and she was desperate to pee. The empty kettle provided a useful receptacle.

Think, Maya, think, she repeated to herself, as she carried the kettle to the far corner and carefully put it down. A roll of duct tape and a bowl of paper clips. What could she do with them?

Opening the paper clips was laborious work. Her fingers quickly became sore; a cut on the palm of her hand opened and blood seeped through the bandage. With difficulty she bent the paper clips into one long wire with a crude hook at the end, then she wrapped duct tape round the stem. It wasn't perfect, it might fall apart, but she had to try to open the lock.

At the top of the stairs she set to work pushing the wire between door and frame. Just as she was poking at the latch, she heard footsteps outside and the door rattled. She fled downstairs, terrified that Omar or Nazim would find the wire.

Breathing heavily, she waited at the bottom of the stairs, heard the scrape of the door and light footsteps running down. She stepped back into the room and Lubna appeared, anxious and breathless.

'Quick!' she said, grabbing Maya's arm. 'I'm

setting you free.'

To Maya's astonishment, Lubna pulled her up the stairs, out of the open door and into the yard.

'Why?' Maya asked, as they ran across the yard and into the bookshop.

Lubna gave her a disdainful look. 'For Khaled,' she said, a warm glow entering her eyes as she said his name. 'Run, leave while you can,' she urged, pushing Maya through the kitchen. 'Go! They're all in a meeting upstairs. Escape before it's too late.'

Letting go of Maya's arm, she ran up the stairs and disappeared. Maya hesitated. She knew she should flee, but she was thinking hard and fast. If she quit, she'd be no nearer to finding her mum than she was before, and she wanted to know what they were talking about at the meeting.

Turning back, she darted into the kitchen, grabbed a small, sharp knife and tiptoed up the stairs. Slowly she crept towards the door of the big room, pressed her ear to the crack and listened. The meeting was in progress, a booming voice filling the room.

'Anyone who suffers for Islam shall be rewarded. Thousands of our Muslim brothers have died, and we shall avenge their deaths.'

This was followed by muttering and cries of

'Allah be praised'.

Then it went silent. At this point Maya knew she should run, but she couldn't move. She was frozen to the spot, her attention riveted. A voice she recognised as Omar's spoke.

'Pamela Brown was going to expose our plot. Now we have her in our power. We must not be deterred, we must complete our mission.'

'We are ready,' voices replied.

There was some clapping and then Omar said, 'Brothers we are—'

Maya leaned closer to the door, straining to listen. If only he'd say where they were hiding her mum, give some sort of clue. Her whole attention was focused on what was going on in the closed room, so she was unaware of somebody approaching from behind. When a hand gripped her shoulder, she almost screamed. She bit deeply into her bottom lip as she was pulled round, and found herself staring into the face of Nazim. His thick eyebrows were drawn together, the silver scar furrowed and wrinkled, he gave her a gap-toothed smile.

'So,' he said. 'Maya Brown. How did you—?'

He didn't get chance to finish his sentence. In one fluid movement Maya grabbed the lapel of his jacket and swept the knife up to his throat. He gasped as she pressed the cold steel against his neck.

'Don't make a sound,' she said threateningly.

His eyes bulged and goggled, he made a choking noise. Then she shoved him backwards and ran for it.

Leaping down the stairs three at a time, Maya ran into the bookshop, rushed over to the door and pulled back the latch. Behind her she heard shouts, but she was away, running up the street and round the corner.

No time to think which way to go, she raced towards a group of women and children and charged blindly through them. In front of her were two men unloading a van. She dodged round them and nearly fell over a box of bananas. Without pausing to think, she dashed across the road and into the Begum Emporium.

Standing behind piles of shiny fruit was the grey-haired woman, Khaled's aunt, who'd directed her to the bookshop.

'Help me,' Maya screeched. 'Hide me, please.'

'Come.'

The aunt reached out, clutching Maya's arm and thrusting her into the back of the shop. She closed the door, leaving Maya in a narrow hallway full of boxes. Leaning against a stack of wooden cases, Maya was wreathed in strong fruity smells, blood pounding in her ears, her breath coming in short, quick gasps.

When she heard raised voices coming from the shop, she flinched and shrank back between the boxes, desperate to know what was going on, yet not daring to move towards the door.

A man shouted, something bumped and fell to the floor, Khaled's aunt yelled. Trying to stifle the cough welling up in the back of her throat, Maya clamped her hand over her mouth, her front teeth digging into the soft skin of her palm.

The voices died away. She dropped her hands and breathed deeply, calming her nerves. The door clicked, a light went on.

'Come with me.'

She was relieved to see the crinkly grey of Khaled's aunt's hair and her big bold eyes peering in.

'Don't worry. They've gone,' the aunt said, putting her hand on Maya's arm. 'That Nazim,' she scoffed, 'always up to no good.'

As the woman ushered her towards some stairs, Maya's heart was still in overdrive, and if it hadn't been for a steadying hand she would have fallen backwards. At the top of the stairs Khaled's aunt darted forward, opening a door into a spacious room which was filled with colour and light.

'Sit down,' she invited her, gesturing to a big, squashy sofa.

Maya sank gratefully onto the soft red cushions. The colours of the room blurred, she leant forward, breathing deeply, pressing her hands down on her legs to stop them shaking. Her brain wanted to shut down. She was panicked, too drained to deal with this woman who was giving her searching looks. All she wanted to do was close her eyes and make everything go away. But the woman had helped her and Maya knew she owed her an explanation.

'I'm Mariam,' the woman said, sitting down opposite Maya. 'And you're the girl I saw yesterday.'

Her voice was deep and musical. Maya remembered it from when she'd given directions to the bookshop, the 'r' sound exaggerated so that the words bounced and rolled.

'I asked you the way to the bookshop,' Maya said.

'Did you find it?'

'Yes.'

'So, why are you running away?'

'Those men wanted to lock me up.'

A startled look crossed Mariam's face. 'Who are you?'

Maya folded her arms across her chest, biting the inside of her cheek whilst thinking hard. Could she risk telling Mariam the truth? Would Mariam be so keen to hide her if she knew who she was? She almost began to lie and tell her she was on the run from her family, but couldn't think of a reason why Nazim and Omar's men would be chasing her. Anyway, Khaled's aunt's keen eyes told Maya she wouldn't be fooled.

Finally Maya took a deep breath, removed her headscarf and shook out her hair. 'I'm Maya Brown. My mother's Pamela Brown. She's head of a government counter intelligence unit. Yesterday she . . . she . . . was kidnapped by . . . terrorists.'

'Oh, my goodness! It was on the news.' Mariam's eyes widened, she put a hand to her throat. 'You're the daughter?'

Maya nodded. 'The men at the Red Moon bookshop – they took her, they're hiding her somewhere.'

Mariam's eyebrows shot up, she looked

completely stunned, her hands gripping both sides of the big armchair while Maya told her the rest of the story.

'A man called Omar Hamed's the leader. The bookshop's a front – he's a terrorist.'

Mariam grasped the folds of her long skirt, then raised her eyes to Maya's. 'I know Omar. He's a local business man. He has extreme views, but I don't know, I can't imagine him kidnapping anybody.'

'He recruits young people – they're his soldiers. They want to be martyrs for Islam.'

'Oh, my God,' Mariam murmured. 'Is Khaled involved?'

'He was helping my mum, sending her information – at least, I think he was. It's hard to know for sure.' She paused thoughtfully, picking at the bandage on her hand. 'He tried to save me from Omar and got Lubna to let me out, so I suppose he must be on our side. But then, he knew about Omar's plan to kidnap Mum and he did nothing to stop it.'

Mariam's hand slipped down to clutch at a half-moon pendant dangling from her neck; her face creased into deep lines. 'Could he have stopped it?'

'No, I suppose not. Well, not without giving himself away.'

'But you thought he might know where they've taken your mother?'

'Yes.'

'Did you talk to him?'

'I didn't have the chance. At first I didn't know if I could trust him, then everything got in a mess. Nazim recognised me and I had to run.'

Mariam's eyes took on a faraway look. 'Khaled hates violence. He hates what the Islamist extremists are doing but . . . actively working against them, that's very risky.'

She let go of the pendant. The crescent moon gleamed softly against her olive skin while she sat twisting and untwisting her fingers, thinking deeply. Then her face sharpened. 'Khaled has a good heart, a keen sense of justice. I can imagine him reporting on Omar if he felt it was justified. But now, if Omar's kidnapped your mother, Khaled could be in great danger.'

Maya tensed. 'It's possible, but Mum won't give him away.'

Every emotion registered on Mariam's face – fear, worry, sympathy. She moved over to sit beside Maya and took her hand. 'I can't believe it, it's almost too much to take in. I'm shocked, horrified – and you, you must be shattered. Dreadful, so dreadful.' She made a soft, clucking noise in her throat. 'And Khaled. If it's true, I'm frightened for him.'

She folded her hands round Maya's and held them tight. 'If Khaled's safe, he should be here soon; he always comes to eat with us. Let's hope he arrives with some good news.' She shook her head and sighed. 'Oh, my dear, this isn't a job for you. Omar's obviously a wicked man.'

'I know. I found that out the hard way.'

'You must be tired. Let me get you a drink. I'll make some tea.'

'Just a glass of water, please,' Maya said.

Mariam's long purple skirt swished as she walked out of the room. Everything about her was warm and bright, and Maya felt comforted. When she'd gone, Maya looked about her and saw how the room reflected the aunt's personality: the walls decorated with tapestry hangings, richly-woven cushions scattered on the red upholstery and, on the floor, beautiful and intricately patterned rugs. Even the smell of the flat seemed reminiscent of her – a heady mixture of spice and flowery fragrance. Maya couldn't believe that when she'd first seen her, she'd thought her plain and harsh-looking.

A tap ran in the kitchen, a door opened and closed and Mariam returned, smiling and holding a glass filled with iced water and lemon.

'Thank you,' Maya said, taking the glass.

Crossing the room to switch on a mock log fire, the aunt brushed some dust from her skirt, straightened her blouse and smoothed back her hair. Her movements were unhurried and precise; she seemed to have recovered quickly from the shock of Maya's news, but seeing her so regal and composed was suddenly too much for Maya. Something in her snapped.

'I want to know why,' she demanded.

'Why?' Mariam asked, puzzled.

'Why Omar's planning to blow up buildings and kill hundreds of innocent people. What's driving him?'

Maya saw Mariam's shoulders tense, she drew in her chin, her eyes were startled. 'Omar's going to plant bombs?'

'Yes. Well, his followers are.'

Mariam blinked. 'Then he has to be stopped.'

'I know. But why? Why does he want to do it?'

Slowly Mariam moved round the armchair, pushed one of the big cushions aside and sat down on the sofa. 'I don't know. I don't understand men like Omar. My religion is one of love, not hate.' She clasped her hands together and sighed. 'Many Muslims came here to escape difficult regimes, they don't want to cause trouble. They want to build a peaceful life, to contribute to society. Unfortunately, it only takes a few Islamic fanatics to give us a bad name.'

'But what they do – what Omar's planning to do – is terrible.'

'Yes, it is. And we all get the blame. 9/11, the London bombings – people look at me with suspicion. They don't understand that I'm afraid too. They move their children away from me in shops and buses. One woman actually spat at me, called me a "Muslim murderer".'

'That's horrible,' Maya said. 'People are ignorant; a boy on the train called me "Paki".'

'I've had to get used to that,' Mariam said. 'And I was born in Turkey.'

Maya leaned her head back on the soft red cushion and rubbed her eyes. 'My family were from Albania,' she said.

'What happened?'

'War.' Maya set her jaw firmly against any further

questions and sat in silence for a moment. Then she turned to look at Mariam. 'If I can find out where Omar's holding my mum, I can get help to rescue her and Omar's mission will fail.'

'I'll help you in any way I can, but you must be careful.'

'I know.'

Mariam put her hand on Maya's arm. 'You love your mother very much, don't you?'

'She's amazing, she. . .' Maya's bottom lip started to tremble. How could she explain what Pam meant to her? Pam who'd rescued her, who'd coaxed her to speak after weeks of silence, who'd fought to adopt her after having chosen to have a life without children.

'Is there anybody you want to phone?' Mariam asked.

Maya nodded. 'I have to contact Simon.'

'Use the phone in the hall.'

Slowly Maya got up, but when she held the phone in her hand, she realised it was Khaled she needed to talk to. When she had the information Pam wanted, then she'd phone Simon.

Mariam paused as she went through to the kitchen. 'Did you get through?' she asked.

'No. He wasn't there.'

'I'm going to get food ready. Will you eat with us?'

Maya nodded, although she didn't feel much like eating.

Before she walked away, Mariam put her hand lightly on Maya's shoulder. 'Don't forget,' she said, 'we're not all terrorists.'

'I know,' Maya answered. 'But I still don't understand why people like Nazim want to blow up innocent civilians.'

'I'm sure he could give you many reasons,' Mariam said. 'We'll talk about it at dinner. But you're tired. You need a rest.'

Holding Maya's arm, she guided her back into the sitting room and over to the sofa. Picking up a throw from the armchair she tucked it round Maya's shoulders. 'There, it's growing cold.'

Maya leaned back into the corner of the sofa. In the warmth of the cosy sitting room it was almost possible to believe the kidnapping had been a horrible dream. She thought of Helen back at the cottage, and then her mum. She hoped they knew she was thinking about them and sending them love. Sliding a big cushion under her head, she settled against the arm of the sofa. For the moment she felt safe. She just had to stay strong, and when Khaled came, perhaps he'd have some news.

Her eyes closed and she sank into an uneasy sleep.

Chapter Sixteen

Waking with a start, Maya found three other people in the room: Mariam pouring tea, Khaled opposite her in an armchair, and a bearded man standing near the door. The man was holding a plastic carrier bag and looked as if he'd just come in. Maya eyed him suspiciously, but as she uncurled herself and sat up Khaled introduced him as his uncle Ali, Mariam's husband.

'Soraya wants to learn how to be a good Muslim,' Khaled told him. 'She's studying at the centre.'

A look passed between Khaled and his aunt. Maya reached for her headscarf, arranging it as Lubna had taught her and tucking her hair underneath.

'She has nowhere to go tonight, so she's staying here,' Mariam said.

Uncle Ali smiled. 'Always taking in strays,' he said, patting his wife affectionately. He turned to Maya. 'I'm pleased to meet you. Will you make *salah* with us?'

Maya blinked and hesitated. She didn't know what *salah* was, but she said, 'Yes, of course.'

'Then we must wash,' Mariam said. 'Come with me.'

When the women returned, Uncle Ali had laid four prayer mats out on the floor and he and Khaled had put on small white hats. Following their example, Maya removed her shoes, stood to attention and raised her hands to the side of her head.

'*Allahu Akbur.*'

The lilting words chanted in Uncle Ali's rich tones were hypnotic.

'*Ashaduan la ilaha illa hlah.*'

The phrases were repeated, flowing softly, gaining power, soaring, then falling to a whisper. Their clothes rustled as they moved from standing to bowing, to kneeling; the age-old words resonating in the room filled Maya with peace and hope. She closed her eyes and let the words flow through her. 'There is no God but Allah. Muhammad is the messenger of God, praise be his name.'

Her eyes opened as the other three fell forward in unison, pressing their foreheads down until they touched their prayer mats. There was something mysterious and yet so simple and unaffected about their devotion, that Maya envied them their faith and certainty.

Everything is God's will, nothing is random, everything is an integral part of God's eternal plan. Muslims don't ask God for anything, because what happens is fate.

Maya remembered Lubna's words, but she couldn't help asking and praying fervently, 'Please let it be God's will that I find my mum, please God, let me find her alive and well'.

Uncle Ali's last words faded and shivered in the corners of the room. There was a soft, fluttering silence, then Mariam rose to her feet. She stood for a moment, head bowed, before walking over to the door. 'Now we'll eat,' she said, and went out of the room followed by her husband.

Maya, still kneeling, watched as Khaled began carefully rolling up the prayer mats, his hands moving in precise, familiar patterns. She shuffled to one side so that he could take hers, leaned back, then moved up onto the sofa. When the mats were stowed away he sat down, and Maya was aware of his eyes on her.

'You've caused me a lot of problems,' he said.

'I've *got* a big problem,' she shot back at him.

'I know, but you should have waited. These things cannot be rushed.'

'That's what everybody says.'

Khaled looked down at his hands resting in his lap, then back at Maya. 'It's imperative that Omar trusts me, and now you've muddied the waters. He's suspicious, and that makes it more difficult and dangerous for me to operate.'

Maya was unfazed. 'My mum thought she could trust you.'

Khaled clicked his tongue impatiently. 'My mission is to stop Omar's plans.'

'But you knew they were going to kidnap my mum. Why didn't you stop them?'

'And give myself away?'

Maya could see his point. She leaned back on the cushions, her eyes were still heavy with tiredness, but there were important questions she had to ask.

'Where do you think Omar's taken my mum?'

'I don't know.'

'But Lubna told me you're one of the leaders, you must know.'

'I don't.' He pulled irritably at the collar of

his shirt, then leaned forward clasping his hands. 'Omar's happy for me to run the bookshop, to be the respectable face of the Brotherhood, the teacher, but I'm not one of his soldiers.'

Maya stared into his green eyes, as though trying to see into his soul. 'Your photo is marked,' she said. 'You're one of the suicide bombers.'

He sighed. 'A way to make Omar trust me.'

Maya understood what a dangerous game Khaled was playing. If Omar discovered his betrayal, he was a dead man walking. She had a sudden, urgent thought. 'Will Lubna give you away?'

He smiled. 'No, I made sure of that.'

Maya didn't ask him how. She'd seen the way Lubna acted around him, but she was worried for her safety. 'What if Omar finds out she set me free?' she asked.

'Lubna's a valuable soldier. They won't hurt her. She'll be re-educated.'

Sinking back into the sofa, Maya tried to think what she should do next. It was still light outside, a summer's night, but the street lamps were glowing yellow and time was passing, using up her chances. She turned and looked at Khaled. 'Will you help me rescue my mum?'

He spread his hands, palms upwards. 'First, we have to find out where she is. Then we have to act quickly, before they persuade your mother to give the name of her informant.'

'Mum won't tell, not unless they. . .'

Under the thick dark lashes Maya's eyes were full of alarm.

Khaled nodded. 'My life, your mother's life and those of many others hang in the balance. We have to find her quickly. You have to be brave. We all have to be brave.'

Maya looked over at the rolled prayer mats, her eyes stinging with unshed tears.

Please keep Mum safe, please don't let them torture her, she prayed. Briefly she closed her eyes, but the horrible images from her dreams came back to haunt her. She blinked and shook her head, and was relieved when the door opened and Mariam came in.

'Go and wash,' she said. 'Food's ready.'

On the table a feast was spread. Maya couldn't imagine eating anything, but when she sat down Mariam coaxed her with delicious pastries, savoury rice and small fragrant pieces of meat, until, despite all her worries and the aching tiredness, she began to enjoy the food.

Uncle Ali poured tea for her and gently persuaded her to take more, praising his wife's cooking. 'Come, come, you are a guest. Try some of this. Nobody makes this like Mariam – it's delicious.'

His hospitality was hard to refuse and Maya ate hungrily.

'So, Soraya. . .' Uncle Ali said.

Maya started. She'd almost forgotten her adopted name.

'You want to learn how to be a good Muslim?'

'Yes.'

'First, you have to give up some of yourself, to learn humility.' He munched slowly, leaning over the table. 'You've been brought up in the West. Yes?'

Maya nodded. 'Yes.'

'Then it won't be easy for you. Western society is based on money, commercialism, greed – everybody out for themselves. That's not the Muslim way. A Muslim is one who submits to God's guidance by obeying His laws; he learns to think of God first and himself last.'

'I understand,' Maya said.

'A Muslim lives by the Divine Decree.'

'And does that include killing and fighting?'

As soon as the words were out of her mouth,

Maya knew she'd made a mistake. It had been a stupid thing to say, but she was so tired. Khaled shot her a warning look, his face clouded with anger, his green eyes flashing.

It was Mariam who smoothed things over. 'Soraya was asking me why some Muslims are militant extremists.'

Uncle Ali put down his spoon and wiped his fingers on a napkin. 'The reasons are complex. It is partly to do with history, going all the way back to the time of the Crusades, when Christians invaded Muslim lands. Throughout time Britain has been an aggressive nation, plundering and conquering, drawing lines on a map, dividing people; causing suffering and conflict in Ireland, making thousands of Palestinians into refugees by creating Israel.'

'But that's all in the past,' Maya said.

'You think so?' Uncle Ali said. 'Palestinians are still being abused, denied basic human rights. And recently Britain joined the US to invade Iraq.'

'But that was to help the Iraqi people.'

'Perhaps, but many didn't see it that way. They thought it was more about the control of oil.'

'And it hasn't helped Iraq?'

'Not really.'

'So, is that why young Muslims feel angry?'

'Partly. There are many reasons – social and cultural. Young Muslims have big identity issues. Tradition dictates they honour the old ways, yet the Western way of life is attractive. Then, every day on the news there are images from the Middle East – fellow Muslims living in poverty, being blown up. All these things create tension.'

Maya felt her head beginning to whirl, the food on the plates started to bob and dance. Uncle Ali's tie became a swirling pattern of yellow and purple. She struggled to concentrate on what he was saying but his words faded and her eyes started to close.

Mariam's voice startled her. 'Ali, I think you've said enough. Soraya's very tired.'

Maya blinked and shook her head. 'Sorry. I didn't get much sleep last night.'

'I apologise,' Uncle Ali said. 'I'm apt to get carried away when I start talking.' He let out a roar of laughter and despite her worries, Maya laughed too.

The rest of the meal passed in light banter between Mariam and her husband. Khaled joined in, but mostly he was quiet, and a few times Maya caught him looking off into the distance, a brooding expression on his face.

It wasn't easy for Maya to sit out the meal. She constantly looked at the clock on the wall, aware of time passing, feeling she should be doing something. When Mariam rose to clear the table, she was glad to move and offered to help.

They carried dishes through to the kitchen and while Mariam ran hot water into the sink, she asked Maya about her life at home. The questions were difficult to answer because it seemed to Maya she had no life other than this aching mess of confusion. She couldn't believe that Helen was back at the cottage in Derbyshire, just a couple of hours away. It was like a life she'd left years ago.

When Mariam saw that her questions were causing Maya pain, she steered her back to the sitting room where Khaled and Uncle Ali were watching TV.

'You settle down there and I'll make up a bed for you,' Mariam said. 'I won't be long, then you can sleep.'

Film credits scrolled down the screen as Maya nestled on the end of the sofa. There was a trailer for a travel programme, then the kidnapping of Pamela Brown was headline news. The Home Secretary appeared, warning the public to be vigilant.

'The country is on critical alert,' he said. 'Intelligence officers warn that terrorists are planning to bomb tourist attractions throughout Europe.'

He was replaced by a reporter telling of a breaking news story.

'Security Forces are surrounding a farmhouse in the Buckinghamshire countryside where it's believed terrorists are holding Pamela Brown, the top security expert who was kidnapped yesterday morning.'

Maya leaned forward, her attention riveted. Her stomach twisted into knots as the camera panned across a row of police marksmen. A close-up of the farm filled the screen.

As Uncle Ali denounced the terrorists, Maya looked across at Khaled. Had she been following a false trail? Had he deliberately double-crossed her?

She watched as the police marksmen waited. The TV camera zoomed up to the doorway.

'It's believed five gunmen are holed up in the farm guarding Ms Brown. A specially trained intelligence officer has been negotiating with the terrorists for Ms Brown's release, but so far it's thought that the terrorists' demand for safe passage to a country of their choice has been denied. The fear is, of course, that if security forces storm the building, the terrorists will simply blow themselves up *along with their captive.'*

The camera panned round the farmhouse again. Maya fixed Khaled with a deadly stare. If he had lied, she swore to herself that she'd kill him.

It was a stand-off at the farm, with no action to capture, so the camera switched back to the newsroom and another dreadful story – a bomb had gone off in Bali. Reports about the victims made Maya want to cry. She looked at a photo of a young medical student who'd just finished her final exams and was on holiday celebrating with friends. Her mother brokenly described her beautiful daughter and said how proud the family was of her. 'The first girl in our family to go to university and she was soon to be a doctor.'

How could the terrorists do it? How could they not care? How could they see young people out enjoying themselves with all their lives in front of them and blow them up?

Uncle Ali was furious, practically spitting at the television. 'These terrorists are not Muslims. They are murderers,' he said vehemently.

Vaguely Maya was aware of Mariam coming into the room. 'I've made the bed up in the spare room. Whenever you're ready, Khaled will show you where it is.' Then she turned to her husband. 'We have to cash up,' she said.

Uncle Ali, still muttering, followed his wife out of the room.

As soon as they'd gone, Maya fired a question at Khaled. 'Are you sure my mum's not in that farmhouse?'

He raised his eyebrows. 'Security forces have been known to be wrong.'

'I don't want to play games. I want to know. Is my mum here in Leeds?'

'Yes. She's here.'

'How do you know for sure, if you don't know where she is?'

'I know they brought her up to Leeds. Omar boasted at the meeting that she was his prisoner.'

'Have you seen her?'

'No, of course not.'

Maya's mind was going round in circles, she didn't know what was true any more. Eyeing him suspiciously, she asked, 'Was it you who gave her away? Did you get Omar's men to kidnap her?'

Khaled's eyes widened. 'I was trying to help her!' he said indignantly.

'You pledged yourself to kill.'

'I'm not a killer. I had to volunteer. It was the only way to convince the Allied Brotherhood I was one of them. It's the ultimate sacrifice – to die for the glory of Allah, praise be His name.'

'Would you do it – would you plant a bomb and blow people up?'

'Of course not. I was counting on your mum to disrupt our plans. I was giving her information, remember?'

'Yes, I remember. Information about destruction, plots to blow up innocent people.'

'But are they innocent?' Khaled countered. 'Did the British do anything when their government invaded Iraq, when they interned Muslims without trial?'

'Whose side are you on?' Maya challenged.

Their eyes met, full of anger and bitterness. Khaled sighed. 'Sometimes I'm not sure,' he said. 'Thousands of Iraqis were killed when your country and the US invaded.'

'England's *your* country too,' Maya said quietly.

They both fell silent, watching the TV that had flashed back onto the farmhouse surrounded by police. Maya tried to work out how the fact that the Security Forces thought her mum was inside the farmhouse changed things.

Khaled seemed to read her mind. 'The siege at the farm gives us a bit more time,' he said.

'How do you mean?'

'Omar will have a false sense of security.'

'Yes, but he knows I'm free and searching for my mum.'

'With respect, he's probably less concerned about you than about the Counter Terrorism force. He'll know that their resources are concentrated on the farm at the moment, so he won't be expecting a rescue attempt.'

'Haven't you got any idea where my mum is?'

'Not yet,' Khaled said.

Maya sat back, thinking. An image came into her head. The advert in the newspaper for Omar's carpet sale with the word CANCELLED stamped across it.

'Is Omar a good businessman?'

'I guess so. He makes a lot of money.'

'So why do you think he put an advert in the paper for a sale at his warehouse, then cancelled it?'

Khaled shrugged. 'I don't know.'

Maya jumped up. 'It's because that's where he's got Mum – in his warehouse on Queen's Street.'

Khaled looked sceptical. 'That's too easy and

it's too public.'

'How far away is it?'

'A few streets.'

'I'm going there.'

'That's madness. There's no way your mum is there. And if she was, she'd be guarded.'

'I know. I need a gun.'

Khaled looked at her. 'You think one girl with a gun is going to beat Omar's men?'

'Yes. Can you get me a gun?'

'You can't do this.'

'Tell me how to get to Omar's warehouse. Have you been there? Do you know the layout?'

Khaled hesitated. Maya moved closer, staring at him challengingly. He looked down at the floor, then met her gaze. 'All right. I'll tell you everything I can, but you have to promise me you'll wait for the right moment. If you go without a plan you'll screw everything up.'

Maya gritted her teeth and glared at him. 'I'll wait – but not for long.'

Chapter Seventeen

Heavy banging on the shop door below sent Khaled rushing to the window. He peered out.

'Omar's men.'

Mariam came scuttling into the room, followed by Uncle Ali.

'What's happening?' she shrilled.

'It's Omar's followers,' Khaled told her.

Uncle Ali started to rant. 'What do they want? Thugs! Omar always thinking he's such a big man.'

'Be quiet!' his wife told him. 'Quick,' she said, pulling at Maya's arm. 'Come, I'll hide you.'

Uncle Ali's eyes were wide with surprise as Mariam hustled Maya across the landing and opened the door of a narrow cupboard. While Khaled ran downstairs, she shoved Maya inside and slammed the door.

Maya held her breath as footsteps stamped into the shop below, then several sets of feet tramped up the stairs. Her heart stopped as they passed in front of the cupboard door. Somebody spoke loudly, a door banged, then the sound of voices faded.

She waited, her pulse racing, her breath trembling in her throat. Would Omar's men search the place and find her? Mariam and Uncle Ali had no reason to protect her – if they gave her away, she'd be back in Omar's clutches.

A door opened and footsteps went into the kitchen. She heard the sound of water running, a kettle being filled, the clink of glasses. Inside the cupboard she was squashed at an odd angle, surrounded by coats, long brushes and bulky things she couldn't quite see. Her back was aching, her neck stiff, but she dared not move a centimeter.

Light footsteps tip-tapped from the kitchen. A rattle of china and a drifting smell of onion and garlic told her that Mariam was sweetening Omar's men with food and drink. A door banged shut. Now she couldn't hear anything except the buzzing of what she thought was a refrigerator or ice chest behind her. She tried to look at her watch, but it was too dark. She tried to breathe deeply but it was hot and airless, suffocating. Almost at breaking point, she distracted herself by humming a tune in her head.

Edging her toe slightly forward to relieve the pressure in her legs, she felt something near her shift and bump. Panic swilled in her stomach like cold soup; at any moment she'd be discovered. Her ears were on stalks, swivelling to pick up the tiniest sound. The click of a door sounded, then voices and footsteps going down the stairs, and finally, the welcome bang of a door below.

She hoped it was Omar's men leaving, but nobody came to release her. It had all gone quiet. What the hell was going on? She was just beginning to think she'd risk opening the cupboard door herself, when there was a rustling outside and light flooded in.

Mariam stood there looking flushed and relieved. 'Come. They've gone.'

Maya staggered out onto the landing, her legs tingling with pain. She bent to rub them, and when she straightened up, Mariam was staring past her into the cupboard.

'I'm so sorry you were stuck in there with all that paraphernalia,' she said. 'You must have been half-suffocated.'

'No problem,' Maya replied. 'It was the least of my worries. Thanks for hiding me.' She looked towards the kitchen. 'Where's Khaled?'

A frown furrowed Mariam's face. 'He's gone with them. I listened at the door while they were talking. They told him he had to help find you. They said, if he doesn't find you and hand you over to them, he'll regret it.' She clasped her hands. 'They blame him for letting you into the bookshop. They're frightened you know too much and you'll go to the authorities. Omar's men are not to be trifled with.'

'I'm sorry,' Maya said.

'You cannot help it. It's them. They're in the wrong. They are evil.'

'Thank you,' Maya said.

Mariam took Maya's hands in hers. 'It's all right. Khaled's clever. He'll think of something.' Pulling Maya forward, she guided her into the kitchen.

'Did they say anything about my mum – where she is?' Maya asked.

'They were laughing about the Counter

Terrorism forces looking in the wrong place.'

'Did they say she's here? Did they say anything about the warehouse?'

'They have her, but they didn't say where. Soon they might move her to a safer place.'

Maya threw herself back against the kitchen wall in despair. 'I've got to find her, or she'll disappear forever.'

Mariam pulled Maya to her and hugged her. 'We'll get her back. Khaled will help.'

'Will he?' Maya asked.

'Yes. He's a good boy.'

'Why should he risk his life?'

Mariam held her at arm's length. 'Because he cares,' she said.

Maya closed her eyes for a moment. She wanted to think, but everything span round in her head. She blinked, and blew out a long stream of air. The past two days seemed like a lifetime. When she opened her eyes the red walls of the kitchen blurred and danced.

Mariam patted her shoulder. 'You need some sleep.'

'No,' Maya protested. 'How can I sleep?'

The grey-haired woman smiled softly. 'Come.

There's nothing you can do tonight. Your bed is waiting. If Khaled returns, I'll wake you.'

* * *

Even though Maya was exhausted, she slept only lightly, dogged by dreams of running through woods, guns shooting at her from every side. Somebody grabbed her and threw her into a deep pit. She fell down and down until *bump* – she woke with a start as Omar's face loomed over her. He was holding a dagger.

'I'm going to chop off your finger,' he said, laughing uproariously.

She sat up and looked into the darkness. There was nobody there, but Omar's hollow laughter echoed round the room. She pulled up her knees, shivering violently. She didn't know how long she'd been sleeping, but she couldn't afford to waste precious time. Swinging her legs out of bed she stood up, ready for action, but then common sense kicked in – what, she asked herself, could she achieve in the middle of the night, wandering around a strange city?

With resignation she sat down again, then lay

back and snuggled under the duvet. Lying on her side, she wondered if her mum was asleep. And Helen, poor Helen – she'd be frantic. It was unthinkable that her daughter had been abducted and now her granddaughter was missing, too.

Maya needed to make a new plan, but it was hard to stay awake. Then she heard a definite creak outside the room. The door handle squeaked. Somebody was coming in.

'Don't say anything.'

She sat up; a shadow was moving towards her.

'Don't speak.'

Her mouth opened in a soundless scream. The figure moved closer.

'I shouldn't be here in this bedroom. I apologise.'

Recognising Khaled's voice, Maya relaxed, breathing out a long sigh of relief.

Khaled stood next to the bed and bent down, whispering, 'Omar's very angry. You know too much about his organisation and his plans. He's ordered me to find you and hand you over to him.'

'You won't, will you?'

'Yes. That's exactly what I'm going to do.'

Chapter Eighteen

'But you can't,' Maya shrilled into the darkness.

'I have to,' Khaled said. He sat down on the bed and leaned forward, speaking quietly yet urgently. 'If I give you to Omar, it'll prove my loyalty. He'll think I'm still true to the Brotherhood.'

'So, I'm to be your sacrifice?' Maya demanded.

Khaled's eyes gleamed like dancing stars. 'Omar wants fame. He's masterminding the biggest act of sabotage the world has ever known. If he brings it off, he'll be the undisputed leader of the AB in the Western world.'

Maya pulled up her legs and sat tall. 'The Circle of Fire – bombs all over Europe.'

'He has a new plan to blow up twelve planes simultaneously.'

'My God!' Maya cried.

Khaled put a finger to his lips. 'Shush! You'll wake my aunt.' He waited a moment, then continued. 'Arms and explosives are being shipped to him. Twelve young men and women have pledged to plant and detonate the bombs.'

'And you're one of them?' Maya asked.

'Yes – which makes me part of Omar's inner circle. The information I find out and pass on will save hundreds, perhaps thousands of lives.'

Maya leaned back against the headboard, she could see the way his mind was working. 'So, rescuing my mum isn't a priority any more?'

'No. I'm sorry. This has become bigger and more desperately important than the fate of any one person.'

'I'll give you away. I'll tell Simon you're a terrorist,' she threatened.

Khaled sighed. 'It won't work. Simon knows everything. He's approved my plan.'

'Including handing me over to Omar?'

'Yes.'

Maya felt as if she'd been thumped in the stomach. Her eyes goggled. 'He can't have.'

'I'm sorry.'

Maya stared up at Khaled, waiting for him to give her some hope, to change his mind, but he didn't. His green eyes glowed back at her full of conviction and fervour.

'Your mother would make exactly the same decision,' he said softly.

Maya looked at him in horror. Was he right? She didn't know. She was so frightened, she couldn't think. She wanted to scream at him. She could hit him, knock him out – she had to do something – but her voice was strangled, her limbs frozen with fear.

Khaled bit his lip and looked away. 'The decision's been made.'

Maya glared at him with all the energy she could muster. 'When?' she managed to croak.

'Tomorrow – after midday prayer.'

'I . . . I . . . won't stay here. I'll run away.'

'I don't think so. It's your decision, but I don't imagine you want the blood of hundreds of innocent people on your hands.'

She took in a big gulp of air, heaving and choking as if it were her last breath. For a moment she covered her eyes. 'You can't, you can't do this to me.'

'He leaned forward, his face close to her;

189

everything blurred and she was lost in a pool of green light. She could smell his skin, salty and sweet at the same time. He put his hand on her shoulder. 'Maya, I. . .'

She didn't let him finish, but pushed him away. Light as a cat, he crossed the room and she saw his tall, slim figure silhouetted in the doorway.

'Khaled!'

'Yes?'

'There has to be another way.'

He half-turned, and in a shaft of light she saw his hand rise, his palm turn upwards, his fingers spread – then he clenched his fist. 'It's out of my control,' he said.

The door closed behind him. Maya blinked into the shadowy darkness. She could hardly believe what she'd heard – Khaled was handing her over to Omar, and Simon had agreed to it. Nobody would try and rescue her or Pam. They were to be sacrificed so that Khaled could prove his loyalty and save the world.

She lay back shivering in terror. There was no lock on the door, she could escape, she could go back to Gran. She didn't have to stay. In a few seconds it could all be over – slipping silently down the stairs, out into the street, making her way towards the station. Bright lights, the safety of the train, the cover of darkness, then the warmth of the cottage.

* * *

The night was long. Maya tossed and turned, fretting and searching for an answer. She could see Khaled's reasoning. Of course he had to prove his loyalty to Omar. It was the only way he could obtain vital information – where and when the bombs would be detonated. The security services would act quickly, round up all the main players, disrupt their plans. But surely there was another way to get information? Simon's team could bug the bookshop, infiltrate Omar's meetings. Weren't they supposed to be trained in all the latest espionage techniques?

Lying on her stomach, she clutched at the pillow, pushing her face into its feathery softness. Inside her head two voices were arguing.

'Get out now, he's given you a chance, they're not coming for you until morning. Get up! Go!'

Then a moment later another voice told her, 'You can't run out on Khaled. Omar has to trust him. That's the only way to stop the bombs.'

'And you have to rescue Pam. You have to finish what you started. You haven't come this far to give up without a fight.'

On and on the voices hammered. She'd never felt so lonely. Finally, with relief, she slipped into an uneasy sleep.

* * *

Sounds from the busy street filtered into the bedroom. Maya woke with a sense that something was wrong, something was pressing down on her. Her limbs were stiff, her muscles tight, her hands clamped together. She sat up, stretching, wiping the sleep from her eyes.

Everything is Allah's will, nothing happens by chance.

It was as if somebody in the room had spoken the words – they resounded inside her head, calming, comforting. She didn't know where they'd come from, she wasn't sure if she believed in any god or prophet or spirit, but suddenly she was filled with hope. After all, hadn't she accessed the Red Moon file, found the bookshop, made contact with Khaled, escaped Omar, found refuge with Mariam? All these things had happened, and had brought her closer to finding Pam. She must stay strong, she must have faith – everything would work out.

Rolling over, she sat up, rubbed at her sore shoulder and swung her legs out of bed, then, grabbing her jeans and T-shirt, she went across to the bathroom. Although she'd have loved a long, hot shower, she made do with a quick splash; she had to be alert, waiting, listening.

Out on the landing, she stiffened as the door from the shop opened below and footsteps rapped on the stairs. Relief flooded through her when Mariam appeared.

'Ah, you're awake. Come, I've made some lemon tea.'

In the corner of the kitchen a small TV flashed out news – a Hollywood actor getting divorced, environmental protesters arrested at a power plant, and in a moment they were going to bring viewers up to date with the latest on the search for the kidnapped Security Chief and her daughter.

Mariam and Maya watched and waited while adverts for soap powder, cars and toys flashed across the screen.

'With all my heart, I'm hoping they've

rescued her,' Mariam said.

Maya could hardly speak. Gripping the warm mug with both hands, she watched as pictures of Special Forces wearing breathing apparatus and body armour came up on the screen. A full assault on the farmhouse was taking place: officers advancing with guns and riot shields, billowing smoke, buildings ablaze and two men running out of the burning house, holding up their hands and fleeing towards the camera. A close-up showed one of the men with a blackened face being seized by an officer, his hands forced up his back and handcuffed.

'Bomb-making equipment was found at the farmhouse, but there's no news yet of Counter Terrorism Chief Pamela Brown, who was taken hostage by terrorists two days ago, or of her fifteen-year-old daughter. The raid by Security Forces did not reveal their whereabouts and intelligence sources now believe that Ms Brown and her daughter are being held by another cell of the Allied Brotherhood in the Leeds area.

Suddenly she was aware that Mariam was speaking to her and she hadn't heard a word.

'Sorry?'

'I think you should let somebody know where

you are,' Mariam repeated, switching off the TV. 'You have to let people know you're safe.'

'They know,' Maya said. 'The ones who matter know.'

Mariam reached into a cupboard, took out a big mixing bowl and set it on the worktop. She gave Maya a warm smile. 'I think your mother is close by. You'll be reunited, I'm sure of it, and until then you're welcome to stay here.'

Maya thanked her. She watched Mariam's careful unhurried movements, pouring flour and water into the bowl, her hands moving swiftly and surely, mixing and moulding until she'd formed a smooth ball of dough. It would be easy to leave, escape while Mariam was busy. The thought almost carried her away, but she didn't move. Gripping the edge of her chair, she watched Mariam break off a small piece of dough and shape it into a ball; her hands went through practised patterns, patting and rolling. She created a circle of calm around her as she worked. The dough became a smooth, flat circle.

'What do you know about Omar?' Maya asked.

'He's from an old and much-respected family,' Mariam replied.

'Does he have a wife?'

The dough circle spread wider and grew thinner. 'He has a wife and five children,' Mariam answered. Then, with a wry smile, she added, 'All girls.'

'What's he like?'

Mariam picked up the circle of dough and turned it over. 'Omar loves money and power. The first he has – he's very wealthy – but in his mind, a man with five daughters is a weak man. He has to prove himself.'

'Do you think I could reason with him?'

Mariam's big brown eyes told Maya what a ridiculous notion that was.

'Omar doesn't listen to anybody.' She lifted the board and took the rolled dough over to a griddle. As she slapped down the creamy circle, she said over her shoulder, 'Only his father. He lives with him, and everything Omar does is to impress his father.'

'Why?'

The dough sizzled and turned golden.

'His father is a learned man, much revered in our community. Omar wants what his father has – respect – whatever way he can get it.'

Maya's mind was ticking as Mariam turned over the baking bread. 'So even though Omar's rich, his father thinks he's a failure?'

'Yes,' Mariam said, lifting the bread from the

griddle. 'But his father is also very angry. It's a case of mistaken identity. His favourite son, Omar's brother, was arrested and is being held in jail. Majid is a well-respected teacher – an academic. I'm sure he has nothing to do with terrorism. I understand now, they arrested the wrong man.'

'Where does Omar live?'

'In Queen's Street, near his warehouse.' Her eyes narrowed. 'What are you thinking?'

'I'm not sure.'

Mariam stopped what she was doing and gave Maya a warning glance.

'Don't try and oppose Omar. He's a cruel man. Wait until Khaled gets back. He'll have some news.'

Maya nodded, but her mind was working fast. Maybe there was another way.

Holding out a plate, Mariam offered her the bread. 'Roti – it's fresh and very good. You must eat.'

Maya managed a smile. 'Thanks, I will, but I need to go and wash my hands.'

In the bedroom, Maya crossed to the dressing table and took a quick look in the mirror. Picking up a brush she smoothed down her hair, then she caught up the scarf to make her hijab. Bending down, she looked for her trainers. They weren't under the bed where she'd left them. She looked everywhere in the room, opened a cupboard and searched inside, but couldn't find them. They'd gone. She went back across the landing and poked her head into the kitchen.

'Mariam, have you seen my trainers?'

'Yes.'

'Where are they?'

Mariam was stirring some sauce. She put the spoon down and went over to Maya. 'Khaled asked me to keep your shoes. He was afraid you might run away.'

Maya backed away from her. 'What did he say?'

Mariam smoothed back her hair with a floury hand. 'He said you might try to tackle Omar by yourself.'

Maya forced a smile. 'Oh no, that would be suicide.'

Trying to make her movements seem as natural as possible she picked up a warm roti and broke off a piece. It was delicious, fresh and light. She ate it quickly.

'Can I take a shower?' she asked Mariam.

'Of course you can. Help yourself to clean towels, they're in the bathroom cupboard.'

'Thanks.'

Going into the bathroom, Maya turned on the shower, then – shoeless – she tiptoed to the top of the stairs. Just before she went down to the shop floor, she snatched a pair of Mariam's beaded slippers and, holding them in her hand, peeped through the door into the shop where Uncle Ali was serving customers. When he turned his back, she flashed through the shop and out into the street.

Chapter Nineteen

Omar's wife Shameen carried a big pile of neatly-pressed clothes and distributed them amongst the huge suitcases spread out in the sitting room. She was grumbling, a steady stream of complaints issuing forth against the hastily planned trip.

'Why didn't I have more notice? The girls have studying to do. They don't have suitable clothing. I haven't had time to buy presents.'

Omar was sitting on the sofa, studying a map. He looked up. 'You're taking enough presents to fill a bazaar. The charge for excess baggage will be more than my business is worth.'

'Don't talk nonsense,' Shameen replied.

Omar folded the map. 'I thought this would be a happy event for you – to see your family, an opportunity for the girls to see their cousins.' He pouted. 'I'm a thoughtful husband. How many times have you said that you miss your family?'

'But you're not coming with us.'

'I can't spare the time.'

His wife looked disgruntled. 'For some reason, you want us out of the way.'

'That's not true.'

At that moment Jasmina, their youngest daughter, ran into the room holding some shorts. 'I want to take these, but Mila says they're not suitable.'

'She's right. You won't be wearing those, they're far too short. Give them to me,' Omar ordered.

Shameen snatched them from her daughter, screwed them up into a ball and threw them onto an armchair. 'I wish your father was coming with us,' she said to Omar. 'He'd be so helpful.'

'He doesn't have good memories of his final days in Lahore,' he said loudly.

'That was a long time ago. Things have changed now,' his wife answered.

Omar's father, who was in the next room, heard their conversation. He came through and stood in the doorway. 'The authorities have long memories,' he said. 'Anyway, how can I return home when my son's in prison?'

'Omar glared at his father. 'You always bring that up.'

'It's not a small matter. My eldest son has been wrongly arrested and detained. His children are without a father.'

Omar turned away. 'It's not my fault. What have I done? If you want to blame anyone, then blame the security services, the kafirs with their unfair practices, detaining people without evidence.'

His father's face flushed with anger. He shook his fist. 'You were responsible for those inflammatory leaflets. Violence is not the answer to anything.'

'Leave me alone,' Omar snapped, and, with a face like thunder, he picked up the remote and switched on the TV. His wife continued trying to stuff six sets of clothes into six different suitcases, and his father unfolded a newspaper. Omar seemed to be very interested in a programme about the Chinese economy, but grew more fidgety and agitated as he watched. Several times he looked at his watch.

'Where is it?' he muttered.

'What?' his wife asked.

'Be quiet,' he snapped.

He stood up, and then sat down again, turned the volume up, then down, sat back, then sat forward on the big sofa.

'Please can you move your feet?' his wife asked.

'Shush!' Omar ordered. The TV screen flashed. He turned up the volume again and sat forward, his body rigid, his eyes intent on the screen.

'We've just received a statement reportedly made by the hostage Pamela Brown. Ms Brown, who is Head of the Counter Intelligence unit Viper, was seized by terrorists two days ago. The statement was delivered to the BBC this morning. This is what it said:

"I have recognised the just cause of the Allied Brotherhood and deplore the damage inflicted by Western powers on Muslim countries. In my role as Head of the Counter Intelligence unit Viper, I was in a prime position to aid my Islamic brothers. For two years I've worked as a double agent and have passed crucial information to the Brotherhood to help them plan attacks on Europe. I have converted to Islam and am committed to fighting the Holy War in the name of Allah, may His name be praised. No street or building in Europe will be safe until all Muslim prisoners are released and Western armies are withdrawn from Muslim lands."'

Omar rubbed his hands with a broad smile on his face. 'Spot on,' he said.

* * *

The pink beaded slippers were not the most practical footwear for running away in, but at least they fitted. As Maya slipped them on outside the fruit shop, she glanced up and down the street, unsure which way to go. Not towards the bookshop – she should steer away from that direction. Across the road there was a dingy-looking café; she dodged through the traffic and ducked inside.

The man behind the counter eyed her without a smile. When she ordered coffee and toast, he told her to sit down and he'd bring it over. The air was thick with steam. Two men with bushy moustaches were bending over tiny coffee cups, speaking passionately in a language she didn't understand. Maya went quietly to a table by the window which gave her a good view across the street to Mariam's shop.

Shoving a streaked plastic menu aside, she planted her elbows on the table and pretended to study a faded poster of the Blue Mosque in Istanbul, but her eyes darted constantly toward the street.

She became aware of the two men watching her; she couldn't actually see them, but when they stopped talking she felt the heat of their gaze.

What if they were Omar's men? What if they recognised her? How stupid she was to have gone into a café, she should have got clean away while she had the chance, but now she was trapped. If she left too soon, she'd arouse suspicion. The sensible thing to do was to sit tight.

The coffee was black and bitter, the toast like white cardboard, a slick of grease glistening in the middle. Maya nibbled at the edges, checked the street again, and saw Khaled walking fast. Behind him were three men, among them she recognised Nazim. Swallowing hard, she almost choked, dry crumbs spluttering over her hand. Omar's thugs were marching to capture her, disappearing into the shop. So Khaled had carried out his threat, but he wouldn't have his moment of glory. With a shaking hand she set down her coffee cup – now her plan had to work.

Leaving some pound coins on the table, she shot to the door. Looking neither left or right, she dashed down the street. If anybody was following her, she didn't want to know. No time to pause, no time to look back, she hurried towards the crossroads, weaving her way through a group of mothers, toddlers, pushchairs and children.

She rushed blindly down two more streets, anywhere just to get away. Into a street lined with terraced houses, a newsagent's shop on the corner. Schoolchildren on their lunch break were shouting, grasping at crisps and chocolate, a friendly man behind the counter looked unfazed by the clamour.

'Queen's Street? Yeah, I know it, but, it's a walk. Go down this road to the bottom, past the infants' school, carry on over the next two junctions, left at the traffic lights and you'll see it over the roundabout – lots of old buildings and warehouses.'

Maya thanked him, pushed past the school kids and hurried out. Walking fast, she glanced at the traffic. Would Khaled guess where she was heading? Would Omar's men come after her? It was a risk she had to take. Throwing caution aside, she started to run. It was madness to make herself so visible but, as her feet pounded the pavement, excitement flooded through her – it was positive action, real action. She was putting distance between herself and Khaled and, with hope in her heart, running towards her mum.

At the roundabout she skidded to a halt. There was no missing the sign on the opposite side of the road – *Omar's Carpets, Rugs and Antiquities* – white letters on a huge purple banner. She slowed down, stopped and stared. There was a big entrance on the corner, then the building stretched a long way down the road; on the lower part, the old stone walls were blank, but the upper storey was lined with tiny leaded windows. Was her mum inside the building? Was she behind one of the barred windows or crammed inside an underground cell? Maya sent her a mental message: Hold on, Mum. If you're in there, I'll rescue you. I can't, I won't fail.

As she crossed the road, the huge banner burnt a hole in the sky. Underneath it she stepped onto the pavement, just as a black car with tinted windows cruised past. She had the distinct feeling she was being watched as it drove slowly down the road. A shiver ran through her. Was it one of Omar's soldiers, or Simon's spies? She could trust neither.

Making sure it was all clear, she hobbled into the warehouse entrance. Her feet were sore, the pink slippers were not good running shoes. A notice on the door informed her that the warehouse was closed for the weekend. She tried the door – it was locked.

Leaning back against the wall, she tried to think logically but found it hard to focus.

One step at a time, she told herself, take one step at a time. You have to get inside the building before Omar arrives to open up – if you do this, you'll have a chance. There has to be another door into the warehouse – a back door.

Ducking out of the front entrance, she tracked down the side of the building. When she rounded the corner she saw a black furniture van. It was backed up to the warehouse loading bay and the doors of the bay were wide open. Beside the van were a silver Mercedes and a red truck. Was Omar here? Was he inside the building?

Maya dodged behind the wall when she heard footsteps. Two men came out through the loading bay and climbed into the back of the furniture van. After a few moments, she peered round the corner and scanned the scene. Muffled voices and heavy dragging sounds were coming from inside the van. Silent as a shadow, she darted to side of the van and slid along it; the back of the van yawned wide. She glanced up, but couldn't see the men. She had to take a chance. Standing up, she braced herself and dashed through the delivery bay and into the warehouse.

Rolls of carpet, rugs and furniture blocked her way. She plunged into the middle of them, crouching low, weaving through them, her heart hammering. Behind her, she heard the men dragging something down from the van. She threw herself onto the floor next to a giant roll of carpet as they came closer, their footsteps stamping, their breathing loud; they were carrying something heavy. Blood crashed in her ears, the footsteps paused and then continued. A loud voice split the air.

'Take the cargo upstairs. Be quick and make sure you lock the door behind you. We don't want any more problems.'

It was Omar speaking. The sound of his voice turned her blood to ice, she shrank closer to the floor, trying to breathe gently.

He shouted again. 'Hurry up. I want you back down here. We have to search the place. That girl's snooping around.'

Cold sweat trickled down Maya's back. How did he know she was at the warehouse? When had he seen her? Her knees were trembling so violently that she collapsed onto the floor. Flattening herself against the carpet, she listened to clanging and banging noises, voices shouting, echoing, then fading. Then it all went eerily quiet, a door opened and footsteps rapped on the concrete floor – they were coming towards her.

Her fingers dug into the soft pile. She was sure she couldn't easily be seen, but if somebody leaned over the top they'd spot her. She took a deep breath and burrowed into the thick pile, pulling the loose edge over her head. Footsteps closed in, objects around her were moved. A heavy thump on the carpet sent a cloud of dust up her nose.

Please don't sneeze, Maya, please don't sneeze.

Her nostrils contracted, then Omar shouted, 'She must have gone outside. Go and find her.'

Feet clattered past.

It's OK, she thought, they didn't spot me. But she dared not move.

She imagined Omar standing, watching and waiting for her to emerge. Her mind played tricks; his eyes loomed in front of her, boring into her brain, peering into her soul. She tried to stay in control, to lie still, but her skin started to prickle and itch. She grew hot and found it hard to breathe. The carpet was a trap, she couldn't escape – she was suffocating.

Everything went dark, a mocking voice inside her head told her, 'Omar's always one step ahead, you can't beat him.'

Loud, sudden chimes startled her. Her mind snapped back into gear. Omar was answering his phone.

'I know she's not at the fruit shop, I've already been told she escaped. Tell Khaled I want to see him and. . .'

His voice faded as he moved away, and Maya couldn't hear any more. After a few seconds she poked her head out from under the carpet and dared herself to peer over the top. Omar was hurrying towards the loading bay and when he disappeared outside, she stood up.

Glancing back over her shoulder, she edged her way through cabinets and tables, dodging behind a tall cupboard and then creeping forward until she came to a clear space. In front of her were a few metres of open concrete floor and behind, a brightly lit office.

On all fours she crawled to the office. From the doorway, the first thing she saw were CCTV monitors mounted on the wall. Of course, that's how he'd seen her. She should have known the building would be under constant surveillance. On one screen was a clear picture of the front entrance, on another, she saw Omar at the back door, waving his arms about and looking angry. She crawled toward his desk and from floor level scanned the monitors; entrance door, back loading bay, side view, three shots of the warehouse floor, and a view of the office and one blank screen. Was that a secret room? Was her mum inside it? She looked up. The low ceiling in the office indicated a floor above. There had to be stairs somewhere.

Dashing to the door, she glanced back towards the loading bay – there was no sign of the men returning. Her eyes scanned to the side and in the corner she clocked a door. Scooting over to it, she went through to find metal stairs zig-zagging upwards to a narrow landing. Leading off the landing were two red doors. The first one opened into a kitchen scattered with half-eaten food, trays and crockery. In the corner was an armchair piled with blankets. The next door was locked. Desperately she jammed her shoulder against the door frame, but it wouldn't budge.

From below she heard voices and then footsteps ringing on the metal stairs. Her mind told her to move, but she couldn't. The walkway shook as the feet got closer. She squirmed with fear then her survival instinct kicked in and she flew into the kitchen and hid behind the armchair, pulling the blankets on top of her head.

The door of the next room was unlocked, it opened and closed. Faint voices and a banging noise came through the wall, and then a cry. Her nerves fizzed, her ears tingled, straining for every sound. The door closed. Footsteps came into the kitchen.

A man's voice said urgently, 'Quick, it's dripping everywhere.'

'All right,' another man replied. 'There's a first aid box in the cupboard.'

A cupboard door creaked, a tin rattled.

'How did it happen?'

'Sharp nails, like a razor.'

'Here, dry it with this. I'll wind a bandage round it to stop the bleeding.'

Silence, then a tearing sound. Maya tried to breathe under the wad of heavy blankets. Had she heard Mum crying out next door? Had Mum slashed at the injured man with her nails? Hope rose like a balloon.

Mum, I'm here. I'll get you out.

'Right, that'll do,' one of the men said. 'Let's go.

Omar's waiting.'

Maya was almost throwing the blankets aside when she heard feet sliding towards her.

'Give me a minute. I'm dizzy.'

Bump, somebody sat on the arm of the chair right next to her head. She held her breath. The man's body was close, so close. He gave a sudden loud spurt of laughter. 'It was on the news. Did you hear it? The woman announced she was a double agent. Brilliant, eh? Said she'd converted to Islam. You've got to hand it to Omar, he's clever.'

'Will the spooks believe her?'

'They will when they see her in action.'

'What do you mean?'

'Omar's got big plans for her. A train goes up in smoke – big explosion – and somewhere in the wreckage they'll find the bones of Ms Pamela Brown.'

The men laughed. 'Genius, eh? Then, they'll believe her.'

'Will she do it?

'She's got no choice. Omar's threatened to kill her daughter if she doesn't cooperate; told her he had the girl, showed her a ring.'

There was a pause, then the other man replied,

speaking more slowly. 'I don't know about that. I'm not comfortable with hurting the girl. I've got a daughter myself.'

'You can't get sentimental in war – many of our children have been sacrificed.'

There was a sudden thump on the floor, followed by heavy footsteps. 'Come on, we'd better get a move on. Khaled phoned and told Omar the girl's back at the bookshop. She'd better be, or he's for it. Anyway, Omar wants us back there.'

Despite the blankets covering her, Maya shivered; things were getting worse and worse. They were going to make her mum blow up a train! That was outrageous, she'd never do it. Omar was going mad. But, at the same time, Maya knew how much her mum loved her. Would she? Would she do something so terrible to save her daughter's life? Everything was spinning out of control, she felt as if she was holding up the weight of the world. She had to get a message to her mum to tell her that she was free, that Omar hadn't captured her – it was vital.

Outside the room the men's footsteps ran along the landing and rapped down the stairs.

Maya crawled out from beneath the blankets, held her stomach and breathed deeply.

Staying on all fours, she crept out onto the landing. Below, doors were banging, locks clicked. A car engine started up. From the landing window she looked down onto the street below and saw a silver Mercedes sliding past, followed by a red truck.

What a blessing Omar had ordered the men back to the bookshop. Why had Khaled told them she was there? Had he guessed where she was? Was he buying time for her, helping her after all? She had no idea, but his action had given her a bit of breathing space. When the cars disappeared, she turned and hammered on the locked door.

'Mum, are you in there? Mum, it's Maya. I'm here. I'm going to get you out.'

Chapter Twenty

Pressing her ear to the door of the locked room, Maya listened hard, but heard nothing.

'Mum, if you're in there, hold on.'

Her voice echoed along the balcony, but from inside the room there wasn't the slightest hint of noise. Maya pictured her mum tied down, her mouth taped, but there was no way of knowing for sure if she was inside the room. She wondered if the blank screen on the monitor should show the locked room – had it been deliberately turned off?

Racing back downstairs, she pushed through the doors into the warehouse. Her eyes swept over the cavernous space. There were no other rooms, no way down to a basement, nowhere her mum could be hidden, except in the locked room upstairs.

Flinging herself into the office, Maya checked the monitors – nobody was visible in the entrance, at the side of the building or in the loading bay. The last screen was still blank. She pressed buttons underneath it, but nothing appeared.

Omar's desk was overflowing with papers, telephone directories and files. She searched amongst all the stuff, sifting and shoving things aside. In the drawers she found piles of receipts, pens, money and yes, underneath a sheaf of papers there was a bunch of keys. She grabbed them and raced back upstairs. Her fingers were thick and clumsy, excitement fizzed through her like fireworks.

After three tries, she found a key that fitted. 'Mum,' she yelled, as the lock clicked.

The door banged back, she stepped forward and gazed into a room piled with boxes. Desperately, she scanned every corner of the room – nothing but boxes. Disappointment hit her smack in the face. She smashed her fist down on the corner of a box and let out a stream of curses. Then she clenched her fists and told herself, 'This was never going to be easy, you have to stay strong, plan your next move. For a start, what's in the boxes, what's so important that Omar has kept the room locked?'

Sliding her fingers into one of the bigger boxes spewing straw, she burrowed down until she touched something cold and solid. Quickly she brushed aside more straw and saw dense grey metal – then she uncovered the butt and trigger of a submachine gun.

A bitter taste frothed in her mouth. She screwed up her face and swallowed, panic snagged at her skin like barbed wire. She was out of her depth, this mission was far too dangerous. She wanted to run.

For a few moments, she stood trying to quell her nerves and find some courage. She told herself how far she'd come, how much she was finding out about Omar's operation. Squaring her shoulders, she clenched her fingers ready to delve back into the straw. At the side of the heavy gun she touched something lighter, smaller, and pulled out a hand gun. It fitted neatly into her palm.

Those practice sessions at the shooting range were about to pay off. Maya clutched the gun and felt soothed by its solidness, its weight. She seized one of the tightly packed small cartons and ripped open the flaps. Inside was exactly what she was looking for – small calibre bullets. Carefully she loaded the gun, made sure the safety catch was on and zipped it inside her jacket pocket.

Behind her there was only the slightest sound, the soft scuff of a shoe.

She turned, and there was Khaled. He was breathing rapidly, a sheen of sweat on his cheeks, one long strand of hair across his forehead; his face flushed with anger.

'You should have trusted me,' he said.

'Yeah right!' Maya replied, putting her hand in her pocket. 'I'd have been in Omar's clutches by now.'

'I was following orders,' Khaled said tightly.

'Orders that would have got me killed.'

'No. When you'd served your purpose, the team would have got you out.'

Maya's hand closed round the gun. 'You and Simon don't give a damn about Mum or me. You're too busy saving the world.'

Khaled looked down for a moment, then directly at her. 'Whatever you think, we're on your side.'

Maya snorted. 'Do you know what Omar's plotting now?'

'What?' Khaled asked, with wide-eyed innocence.

'He's going to get Mum to blow up a train. He's told her I'm his prisoner and if she doesn't set off a bomb, he'll kill me.'

'I know,' Khaled said. 'How did you find out?'

'Doesn't matter. All I know is, this is totally crazy. I can't handle it. I have to find Mum now and you have to help me.'

'I'm sorry. I can't. I'm calling Omar now to tell him you're here.'

Maya took a step backwards and pulled out the gun. 'I can't let you do that. Put the phone down on that box.'

'Maya, trust me, please! We have a plan.'

'The only person I trust is myself.'

'This is not the best way, Maya,'

She took a deep breath. 'Possibly, but I can't risk it. I have to set Mum free. Put your mobile down.'

Khaled put his phone down on the box and raised his hands. He spoke rapidly. 'By doing this you're putting the whole mission in jeopardy. Please, just do as I say and everything will work out.'

Keeping the gun pointed at his chest, Maya hissed, 'Don't think I won't use this. Tell me where my mum is.'

'She's in Omar's other warehouse, not here – a place where he stores antiques. It's an old mill.'

'Where is it?'

'At the edge of town, near Headingley.'

'Take me there.'

'I can't.'

'You can drive, can't you?'

'No.'

'Well, I can. Come on.'

She moved behind him and pushed the gun into his back. Khaled glanced round at her.

'This won't work, Maya. There are three of Omar's men downstairs. Even if you get past them, how're you going to rescue your mum with one gun?'

Maya looked at him and smiled. 'I'll hold you hostage. Bargain with Omar or Simon or both of them. Exchange you for my mum.'

Khaled turned his hands palms upwards. 'Think again. I'm not that important.'

Maya waved the gun. 'All right. I'll shoot you.'

Khaled saw her face set into hard lines. He knew she'd been pushed to her limits. When he spoke again, his voice was gentle. 'Maya, without my information the Security Forces won't be able to stop Omar's bombs.'

Maya's face turned dark, she glared at him.

'You're not the only one with brains. I have a plan. Help me.'

'I can't.'

'Then I can't let you go.'

'What good will it do if you shoot me?'

Maya shrugged.

'Look,' Khaled said. 'I'll help you escape, but after that, I don't know.'

She held his gaze for a moment, her dark eyes smouldering, full of purpose. She spoke rapidly to him, outlining her plan. His expression softened. He murmured something, then shook his head. 'OK. We'll do it your way.'

With a rush of relief Maya thanked him.

'First, we need extra ammo,' she said, placing a small carton of bullets in his hand. Khaled put them in his jacket pocket, then Maya picked up a compact but heavy cardboard box. 'Here.'

'What's this?' he asked.

'Butterfly clips. The submachine guns will be useless without them.'

'Good thinking – I'm impressed,' he said, as he slipped the box into his inner jacket pocket.

'Right,' Maya said, examining the keys she'd stolen from Omar's office. She pincered a key between her thumb and forefinger, 'Hopefully, this should be the one.'

Downstairs a door slammed. She grabbed hold of Khaled's arm. 'Let's go.'

'Me first,' he said. 'If we're seen, you can come back and hide up here.'

They stole down the stairs as quietly as they could. At the bottom, Khaled opened the heavy door and peered out. A light was on in the office and voices could be heard. He motioned to Maya to stay low and they crouched down, creeping forwards. Quickly and quietly they dodged through the carpet rolls and furniture until they reached the loading bay. The furniture van was still there, backed up to the open door.

'You're not going to drive that,' Khaled whispered.

'Just watch me,' Maya answered, pushing him towards the cab and opening the door. 'Quick! Get in.'

He jumped up, and she followed. The key went neatly into the ignition, Maya put her foot on the accelerator and started the engine. As the van began to move, three men ran out into the yard waving their arms. Khaled threw himself down so he wouldn't be seen and Maya turned the wheel, driving towards the men. Three bodies dived out of her way as the van roared past.

The startled looks on the men's faces stayed with Maya as she drove through the gates and out onto the open road.

Chapter Twenty-one

'Slow down, slow down!' Khaled yelled.

'I can't.'

'Watch that corner.'

Maya put her foot on the brake and rounded the corner on the wrong side of the road, just managing to steer away from a truck coming from the opposite direction.

'Wow! I was on two wheels there,' she said.

Khaled was looking pale. 'Who taught you to drive?'

'I went round a racetrack. It was a birthday present.'

Khaled rapped on the dashboard. 'This is not a racetrack. Slow down. You'll get us killed.'

'Don't worry,' Maya said.

'They're coming after us,' Khaled yelled.

'Where?'

'The red truck, right behind us.'

Maya focused her attention on the road ahead. The van was big, it was like driving a bus, and hard to judge distances.

'You're in the middle of the road,' Khaled shouted.

'So? That means they can't pass us.'

A short distance ahead was a big junction. Maya knew she'd have to slow down but she wasn't sure if she could.

Think, think – gears, clutch, brake.

There was a horrible grinding noise as she tried to find a lower gear, and then the van juddered like an erupting volcano. She jammed her foot on the brake, there was a skidding noise and they stopped with a jolt. Then something hit them with a massive bang.

Maya jerked back from the steering wheel. 'They've run into the back of us.'

'We've got to get away,' Khaled cried, pulling himself upright. 'Run.'

Maya snatched the keys from the ignition, opened the van door and leapt out. When her feet hit the ground she made off with long, loping strides over rough ground towards a building site. Picking her way over scattered bricks and pipes, zig-zagging over the coarse grass, she dodged through scaffolding and into a half-built house. Khaled threw himself into the building behind her. They were both panting hard.

In words that came out in jagged gasps, he said something that sounded like, 'You – in – Olympics?'

Maya smiled. 'Long legs,' she said. 'Have you got the boxes?'

'Yeah.'

'Good.'

'Do you think they saw me?' Khaled asked.

'No. You were away too fast. They're out of it.'

A workman wearing a hard hat came round the scaffolding. 'What you two doin' 'ere?'

'Er . . . somebody was after us. We're hiding,' Maya said.

'Who?'

'A gang of lads, calling us names,' Maya said, giving her most innocent smile.

The man peered out of the building. 'Well, there's nobody about now. You'd best clear out. There'll be hell to pay if the boss catches you.' He was ushering them out, when he noticed the box in Khaled's hand. 'What you got there? You pinched summat?'

'No,' Khaled said quickly. 'It's stuff for my computer.'

Anxious moments ticked by while the man sized Khaled up. He looked as if he was going to challenge him, but then abruptly changed his mind and nodded. 'OK. Well, it's all clear. You'd better scarper.'

'Thanks,' Maya said.

They made their way over the waste ground towards some shops. It was tempting to run, but a police siren sounded behind them and they didn't want to draw attention to themselves.

The cops had been called to a road accident – three men were clambering out of a squashed red truck. They'd rammed into the back of a big black furniture van with gold lettering on the sides – *Omar's Carpets and Antiquities* – the driver of which seemed to have disappeared.

I know a café where we'll be safe.' Khaled said. 'Let's walk through the trees and we won't be seen.'

He pointed to the wood surrounding the building site – a small oasis of trees and thick brambles that hadn't yet been cleared by the builders. They picked their way through the tangled leaves and creepers.

A police car with a blue light flashing whizzed by while they were waiting at traffic lights. Maya leaned close to Khaled, hiding her head on his shoulder. His hand touched her arm, and when the lights changed he gave her a brief smile.

They walked down a street of shabby shops and went into a bright, neatly-painted café where a small, bald-headed man came to greet them.

'Khaled, Khaled,' he said effusively. 'I haven't seen you for weeks. Come and sit down. We have good lamb today.'

Khaled shook the man's hand. 'Thank you, Karim, but we'll just have coffee. This is my cousin, Soraya.'

'Please, please come and sit.'

They sat at the back of the café, their heads close together, talking over the plan intently and seriously. When they were ready to leave Khaled stood up, reached into his the pocket of his jeans and took out a phone.

'Here, I nearly forgot – your mobile. Keep the line free. Use it for emergencies only.'

Maya seized it eagerly. 'So,' she said, 'everything's settled.'

Khaled gave her a lopsided smile. 'It's a crazy

plan, but it just might work.'

'Give me one hour before you tell Simon, and I only want back-up – no heavy metal, right?'

'Simon's not going to like it.'

'The decision's made. By the time you tell him, there'll be no stopping me.'

Khaled put a hand on her arm. 'Maya, are you sure? It's incredibly dangerous. Omar isn't somebody who makes deals.'

'That's why I have plan B. I've got your map. For God's sake, don't forget to open the vent.'

'I won't.'

Khaled took her hand and squeezed it. Maya's heart thumped loudly as she watched him go.

* * *

Omar was having an apoplectic fit, stamping around the office of his warehouse. 'I can't believe it. You let the girl escape?'

'She was driving the big van. It wasn't our fault. She braked hard.'

'So now she can go to the cops and tell them where we are. Where the hell is Khaled? He was supposed to deliver the girl to me.'

Nazim's eyes narrowed. 'You shouldn't have trusted him,' he said.

'Shut up. Let me think!' Omar shouted. 'I know, I'll issue a warning – if the police don't stay away from us, we'll kill the woman.'

'Yeah, nice one,' Nazim said.

'Will they care?' one of the other men interjected. 'You made her say she's a double agent.'

Omar glared at him. 'They'll care. They can't bear defectors, they'll want to bring her to what they call justice.' He pointed a finger at them. 'Now, get moving. Find Khaled. Tell him to clear the bookshop. You three, move all the guns and bomb equipment from here to the mill. And you,' he said pointing at Nazim, 'find the girl.'

* * *

Maya's phone buzzed as she made her way across the wasteland. It was Khaled.

'What's happened?'

'Omar's issued an ultimatum.'

'What is it?'

'He wants safe passage out of the country, to Pakistan, or he'll order . . . he'll give orders to . . .

kill your mum.'

Maya's fingers tightened round the phone, she swallowed hard.

'How long have we got?'

'Twenty-four hours.'

'OK. Then I've no time to lose. I'm on my way.'

Chapter Twenty-two

Pressed back into the shadow of some bushes, Maya scanned the empty road. Opposite her was the warehouse. Omar's Mercedes was parked by the loading bay. Further down the road she spotted his house, just as Khaled had described: a large, brand new, yellow-brick house with wide frosted windows and a grey roof.

Closing her eyes for a brief moment, she wished she were a million miles away. What she had to do was mind-bogglingly scary. She breathed out, puffing air over her face and opening her eyes. The sky was a perfect, beautiful blue; a ladybird crawled along a leaf above her head. *Fly away home.*

I wish, Maya thought, I wish.

Movement at the bottom of the road caught

her eye. A black car with dark windows nosed into the street and drove slowly towards her. Maya's heart stopped.

No, not now, not when I'm so close. Don't interfere, keep away.

Crouching further back, she watched as the car slowed and stopped outside Omar's gates. Dark figures behind tinted glass – Simon's men. She prayed the car doors would stay closed, prayed Khaled would stick to the plan, prayed he hadn't called Simon yet.

Don't get out, don't ruin my plan.

The car engine purred, five, ten, thirty seconds passed, a minute, then the car moved forwards, drove past and carried on towards the roundabout.

Gathering all her courage, Maya untangled herself from the branches and sped towards the iron gates of Omar's home. The gates rattled, the catch was stiff, but it lifted and she darted through.

On the drive stood the furniture van, a big dent in the back. Treading quietly and quickly, she hurried past it, then went down the side path and dodged down behind some tall plants. Just above her head was a tall, narrow window with clear glass. Slowly, carefully, she reared up and stared into the kitchen.

An old man with a grey beard was sitting at a table reading a newspaper.

That must be him – Sharif, Omar's father.

Maya felt for the gun in her pocket, then, stepping in the soft soil to deaden her footsteps, she crept round to the back door. Her breath was hot in her throat, her heart was thundering as she reached out and lifted the handle. The door opened and swung back; softer than a shadow she whipped inside and closed it behind her.

The old man looked up, startled. 'Who are you?'

Maya pulled out the gun. 'Don't move.'

His eyes widened in shock, his mouth fell open, a hand clutched at his chest.

Holding the gun steady, she hissed, 'Don't move, and you won't get hurt.'

He coughed, making a horrible choking sound. Off her guard, Maya stepped forward – it was a mistake. A wiry hand shot out and made a grab for a knife lying on the table. His eyes were fierce and dark, she saw his nostrils flare. The knife blade flashed. She held her breath as they faced each other, the walls of the room closing in around them. She plotted her moves, one quick sideways thrust at his arm, an elbow to his stomach, an arm round his neck.

Then the blade shuddered, his eyelids drooped, his shoulders sagged. He gasped and mumbled something incomprehensible as he slumped forward.

'Sit down,' Maya ordered.

He reeled backwards and sat down. Immediately, Maya rushed to the kitchen door and double-bolted it. Then she ran to the opposite end of the kitchen, zapped down the long hallway and made sure the front door was locked and bolted.

Dashing back to the kitchen she levelled the gun at the old man's chest. 'I'm sorry,' she said. 'I'm not going to hurt you – just listen.'

He looked up at her. 'Who are you?' he whispered hoarsely.

'I'm Maya Brown. Your son, Omar, has kidnapped my mother.'

The old man blinked, looked puzzled, then frowned, his face creasing into a thousand lines. 'Omar?' he gasped. 'He's not capable.'

Maya tense as he leaned forward, watched his fingers scrabble for the newspaper. He held up the front page, displaying the glaring headlines.

'This?' he asked.

Maya nodded.

Sharif looked stunned. 'Omar ... he ... he couldn't have, he wouldn't be able to.'

'You don't know your son,' Maya said firmly. 'He's one of the top men – the head of a terrorist cell of the Allied Brotherhood. They're part of an international terrorist organisation.'

'No,' Sharif said grimly. He bowed his head and seemed overcome. Then he looked up, his bottom lip trembling. 'He sent all his family away on holiday so suddenly, I knew he was up to something.'

'He's going to kill my mum,' Maya said slowly and clearly.

The old man stared, his eyes cloudy and dazed.

Maya continued. 'Omar kidnapped my mum because she found out about his organisation. He has a team of suicide bombers ready to blow up buildings and planes all over Europe. He wants to be the leader of the Allied Brotherhood in Europe.'

As it all came pouring out, the old man sat blinking and shaking his head. He put a hand to his forehead and mumbled words she couldn't understand.

'I have to save my mother,' Maya said, 'and stop the bombs.'

The old man started to get to his feet. Maya waved the gun.

'Put that away,' he said. 'I'm not on his side. He's my son, but what he's doing is wrong.'

He edged round the table, coming closer. Maya watched him like a hawk.

'It's hard to believe,' he said. 'All his rantings and bitterness, but I never thought he'd actually do anything. I thought he was a fool.'

'He isn't a fool,' Maya said. 'He's dangerous. We have to stop him.'

The old man reached out and patted her arm.

'I'll help you,' he said.

Maya looked into his eyes. He stared back at her, open, unguarded.

'How?' she asked.

'Come with me.'

He led her towards the sitting room. She walked with him nervously, wondering if he was trying to pull some trick. He motioned for her to go inside, but just then the sound of heavy banging came from the kitchen door.

'It's Omar,' he said.

'Don't let him in,' Maya whispered. 'Please! Tell him you're all right, but you've lost the key.'

The old man nodded. Holding her breath, she watched him go back into the kitchen. If he opened the door, she was done for.

He was fumbling with the lock. 'I can't find the key,' he shouted.

There was an answering thump on the door. 'Let me in!'

Maya glanced into the kitchen and saw the old man bend down and shout through the keyhole. 'I can't open it. I've locked the doors and I don't know where I've put the keys.'

Some unintelligible words spattered through the closed door, then Omar's voice said clearly, 'A day for losing keys. I'll send the men across. I have to go back, I'm busy.'

Footsteps receded down the path, a shadow passed the kitchen window. Maya jiggled the keys in her pocket, a triumphant look on her face. It was a small victory, but it would buy her time.

Leaning back against the door, the old man wiped his eyes with a handkerchief. 'He'll send his men.'

'Then there's no time to lose,' Maya said. 'We have to go.'

'What do you want me to do?'

'Be my hostage. I'm going to bargain with Omar – your life for my mother's.'

A corner of his mouth turned up, his long beard bobbed. 'Then we'd better be quick,' he said, snatching up a white shawl from a chair. 'Come on.'

Maya pulled Omar's keys from her pocket, slid back the bolts on the door and, grabbing Sharif's arm, rushed him to the van in the driveway.

'Sorry, sorry,' she muttered as she yanked open the van door and shoved him up into the passenger seat.

'It's all right. Go, go, go.'

She slammed his door shut and ran to the gates. Omar had left one gate open, so she only had the other one to push back. She shoved it hard, glancing across the road. No sign of Omar's men yet.

Racing back to the van, she pulled open the door and climbed into the driver's seat. Her fingers were trembling – she couldn't fit the keys into the ignition.

This is it. You can't fail now. Keep calm, Maya. Come on, yes, that's it, that's the one, turn the key.

Her spirits soared as the engine roared into life.

She crunched the van into gear and shot forwards. Narrowly avoiding a gatepost she turned left, wheels skidding, undercarriage juddering. Miraculously the van didn't stall as it shuddered round the roundabout, then jerked uphill until Maya found the right gear and drove smoothly onto a main road. She glanced across at the old man, who looked ashen.

'Don't worry,' she said. 'I've driven it before.'

A lot of traffic was coming towards her; swerving round a corner too fast, they hit the kerb with a bang. Maya cursed. The old man put a gnarled hand onto the dashboard and steadied himself.

She checked the mirror. There didn't seem to be anybody following them so she slowed down, turned down a side street and drove carefully to the bottom junction. She changed down the gears and pulled up quite smoothly to stop in front of a shop.

When she switched off the engine, the old man took out a handkerchief, wiped his forehead and blew his nose. His breath wheezed in and out, his eyes closed. Maya hoped he wasn't going to collapse.

She pressed her hands to her face and sank forward onto her elbows. The clock on the dashboard ticked, the overheated engine cracked as it cooled.

Then she heard the old man chuckle. She looked at him in surprise. What was he up to? He reached beneath his shawl, digging deep into a pocket. He grinned as he held out a mobile phone.

'Omar,' he said, 'will not bear the shame of a girl stealing his father and his van.'

He punched in some numbers and handed the phone to Maya. 'He'll want to do a deal.'

She listened to the dialling tone and then Omar's voice boomed into her ear. 'Abbu. Are you all right?'

She steeled herself to speak calmly. 'This is Maya Brown. I have your father. If you want to see him alive, you'd better listen to me.'

Omar's voice exploded into spattering sounds. 'Wh . . . wh . . . what? Where?'

When his voice faded she said in icy tones, 'You left you father alone in the house. Now he's with me. I have a gun. I won't hesitate to use it. I want you to release my mother. When you're ready to do a deal, you can phone me.'

She switched the phone off and looked across at the old man. He seemed to have recovered; his cheeks were glowing, his eyes glinted mischievously. He seemed to be almost enjoying himself.

'You must be careful,' he said. 'Omar is not to be trusted. His honour is everything. He will fight to the death.'

In the rear-view mirror she saw a black car with tinted windows drive up slowly and stop behind the van. She flinched as the door opened, her eyes riveted to the mirror. She held her breath. Had she been followed? With only the slightest glance at the van, the man went into the shop.

With a heavy sigh of relief Maya started the engine and eased forward – she had to find a hiding place.

Driving slowly through residential streets she found her way back to the building site. The workmen had finished for the day, so she steered the van over rutted ground to the edge of the wood. Carefully manoeuvring the van, she parked it between trees so that it was partly hidden from the road. When she took her foot off the accelerator her arms and legs were trembling. It was hard to believe she'd actually driven along public roads in such a huge vehicle – and that she'd done it twice. She could have had a horrible accident or, perhaps even worse, caused one. And it wasn't over yet, not by a long way.

Sharif was silent, his head lolling to one side.

'Are you OK?' she asked.

The old man roused himself, sat up and looked at her, his face suddenly alert. 'Don't despair. Omar will contact us.'

'When?'

'When the sun goes down he'll make his decision.'

Maya wondered how she could wait so long. Closing her eyes, she leaned back. It was hot, too hot. She heard the old man cough and felt a tap on her shoulder. Gratefully she accepted the bottle of water he was holding out to her. It was tepid, but she gulped it down. When she handed it back he nodded, replaced the cap and said, 'We haven't been formally introduced. My name is Sharif.'

Pulling the shawl from his shoulders, he folded the white fringed square carefully, laid it on the seat beside him and began to talk. He told her about his family, his early life in Pakistan.

'I had a good life. I was professor of Literature at Lahore University. But I was young, idealistic, I believed in democracy. I joined a resistance group in the 1960s. We helped bring down Ayub Khan's military dictatorship.' He paused, looking wistful. 'I was a freedom fighter . . . but ultimately we failed. Then I was hounded from my post by the government.' He turned away, reached for his shawl and dabbed at his face. 'The government in Pakistan is always at war with its people,' he added.

'What about Omar,' Maya asked. 'What happened? Why does he hate the West?'

'I don't think he ever forgave me for leaving Pakistan. Here we became outsiders. In Lahore we had a spacious bungalow, servants, a beautiful garden. What did we come to? A dismal, shabby terraced house. Then my wife died soon after we came here. I couldn't get a job. Omar hated school, was spat at in the street, called a Paki. Perhaps it was too much for him to bear.'

'But your other son, Majid, he's not the same?'

'No. Majid's an academic, devout, honourable. His struggles have made him stronger, determined to succeed, while Omar's hurt has turned to bitterness.'

'But Omar's rich.'

'Yes, but his business methods don't command respect. He has lied, cheated. Everyone knows this – he's not liked in our community.'

'So now he thinks he'll get people to respect him by turning into a terrorist?'

'A twisted way of thinking. It was because of

Omar that Majid was arrested.' The old man bowed his head. 'Majid's lawyer told me. Omar was distributing Islamist leaflets at Majid's college, spreading hate to the students. When the police went to his home, they found suspicious items Omar had left in the cellar. Omar wasn't brave enough to tell them they'd got the wrong man, and Majid would not implicate his brother. So Majid is awaiting trial.'

Suddenly Sharif seemed exhausted. He closed his eyes, his body slumped and shivered with every breath. His eye sockets were dark holes, his brown skin tough and leathery, deep lines etched on either side of his nose.

The hours passed. Maya fell asleep and awoke with a jolt, annoyed at herself for letting her guard down. Anybody could have crept up on them. The old man was still sleeping; he stirred and muttered, but didn't wake. Maya climbed out of the van and went deeper into the wood, squatted down behind a tree and peed. A rustling noise set her nerves quivering but it was only a bird caught in a thicket. She straightened up and stood with her back to a tree while she re-tied the scarf round her head.

When she returned to the van, Sharif was awake.

Almost immediately his phone jangled. He picked it up and held it out to her. When she pressed the button to connect, Omar's voice came through loud and clear.

'Abbu, are you all right?'

'He's sleeping.'

'Oh, it's you.'

'Yes, it's me.'

'You're causing a great deal of trouble.'

'Is my mum all right?'

'She's safe.'

'I want to see her. I want you to let her go.'

'Then you have to release my father.'

'I'll make a deal.'

'Why should I negotiate with you?'

'Because if you don't let my mother go, I'll kill your father. He's here now by my side, sleeping. I have a gun. I could put him to sleep forever.'

The peal of laughter that came through the earpiece shocked her. It was a horrible, evil, twisted sound that made her blood run cold.

'You're not capable of killing,' Omar taunted.

Making her voice as strong and steady as she could, Maya said, 'His fate is in your hands.'

Omar hesitated. She heard him sniff and swallow,

then he said slowly, 'Come to the mill yard at ten o' clock tonight.' He breathed deeply, paused and then added, 'Your mother will be waiting in a silver Mercedes. Release my father, get in the car and you and your mother will be free to drive away.'

Maya's heart leapt. He was giving in, he was going to let her mum go.

'Have you got that?' he asked.

'Yes. I'll be there.'

Maya was so excited that she didn't care when he abruptly cut the connection. She looked out at the woods, her heart singing, congratulating herself on how clever she'd been. What a stroke of genius plotting to kidnap Sharif. But after a few moments her mind began to fill with doubt.

And when Sharif heard what Omar had said, he stroked his beard, thoughtfully. 'If he's letting your mother go, then she is no longer a threat to him.'

'But she knows about his organisation.'

'That's true.'

Maya saw the doubt on his face. 'He won't let her go, will he?'

'No.'

'Will he double-cross me?'

'Yes. I fear he will.'

'Then thank goodness I have plan B.'

Maya felt in her pocket and pulled out a piece of paper. She unfolded it and carefully studied the map Khaled had drawn in the restaurant. Then, turning the paper over, she picked up her phone and punched in the number written on the back.

Chapter Twenty-three

The mill yard was full of shadows. Maya stopped the van at the entrance, checking for a welcoming party. She saw no one, but was sure she was being watched. At the back of the yard she saw a silver Mercedes.

Putting her foot down on the accelerator, she eased the van forward and steered it carefully through the gates, but as she scanned the yard she lost concentration and the van lurched forwards. Slamming on the brakes, she skidded past the Merc and ploughed into a grassy bank. The steering wheel smashed into her chest and the old man half-fell off the seat, trembling and muttering.

Maya reeled back, wincing with pain. 'Sorry,' she whispered.

Cursing her clumsiness, she turned to look back

across the yard and saw the silhouette of a person sitting in the Mercedes.

She used her mobile to call Omar. 'Stay back. I'm walking your father to the car. Only when I see that my mum is OK will I let your father go.'

She unzipped her pocket, took out the gun and pointed it at Sharif.

'That won't be necessary,' he said quietly.

'It's for Omar's benefit,' Maya replied.

'Let's go out the back way,' he said.

'Why?'

'They won't be expecting it.'

It wasn't easy getting him over the seat, but with a bit of help from Maya, Sharif managed it. They edged round an old sofa and shuffled forward in complete darkness to reach the back doors. The old man found the handle and pulled, but the doors wouldn't open.

'The dent,' Maya said. 'The doors are stuck because of the accident.'

She helped him push, and suddenly both doors swung open.

'Stand here,' Sharif said.

Maya stood beside him. He pressed a button, and a hydraulic lift slowly lowered them into the yard. Before he stepped forward, Sharif turned and whispered a blessing in Maya's ear. Then he began to pray, '*Ashaduan la ilaha illa hlah,*' and he continued a low chant as together they walked over to the Mercedes, Sharif in front, Maya's gun pressed into his back.

Over Sharif's head, Maya saw the car and the silhouette of Pam in the passenger seat. Everything else dropped away, nothing else mattered except her mum, her wonderful, lovely mum, there at last, just ahead of her. She gave Sharif a gentle push, stepped round him and plunged forward.

Her fingers were clumsy, scrabbling to open the door. The light came on. The woman at the wheel was wearing a headscarf. She turned and looked at Maya – her eyes weren't soft and grey, they were glittering and green.

Before Maya could react, somebody grabbed her from behind, strong arms circled her and hauled her from the car.

'Where's my mum?' she shouted.

She recognised Nazim's voice. 'Don't worry, we'll take you to her.'

Mad with anger, Maya thrashed and squirmed, just managing to wriggle away. Light blazed in her eyes, shadows flew past her. She pointed the gun, pressed the trigger and fired into the blackness.

There was a rustling behind her, but before she could turn and shoot again a hand gripped her throat, she was hauled to her feet and then she was falling, stars shattered round her head. As she was dragged across the yard, she heard the sound of a helicopter circling overhead.

Thump! She was slung onto a hard bench, the breath knocked out of her. A door clanged shut. She opened her eyes: everything was blurred. Eventually she made out a table, a chair and a small, high window. It was a cold room in the basement.

From outside she heard sirens, a harsh light sliced across the room, then flicked away. She rolled onto her side and pushed herself up. Her throat was dry, her head throbbing and she was overwhelmed with nausea. She retched, and just managed to stumble into a corner before she threw up. Then she sat on a chair and wiped her mouth on her sleeve.

Dragging the bench under the window, she climbed up and tried to look outside, but couldn't see anything except a haze of lights above her. She got down and tried to put a chair on top of the bench but couldn't do it; her head was swimming.

Moments passed, there was a confusion of rattling noises outside. Her head drooped, her eyes were heavy, she lay down, her energy gone.

She hardly moved when the door opened, but suddenly a hand grabbed her and pulled her upright.

'Bitch!' Nazim screamed at her. 'This is all your fault. You called the cops. We're surrounded. Now we'll all die. Nobody will escape.'

He pushed Maya into a corridor. A man dressed in black was standing there, pointing a heavy gun at her. She thought it was her last moment, she thought the final thing she'd see was the barrel of a gun, and somehow, strangely, she didn't care. She stood there shivering, prepared for the bang. But the next moment she was seized and thrown inside another room.

As she fell into the room, she veered into a chair and knocked it over. Putting her hands out to steady herself, she rammed up against a wall. Behind her, she heard Omar's voice.

'Shove Khaled in there too. He'll die, like the traitor he is.'

Maya turned round to see Khaled being led in. As the door was re-locked he looked despairingly at her. 'They found out,' he said.

'I thought you'd betrayed me.'

He dropped his eyes, walked over to the far wall and knelt down. There was somebody lying on the bed underneath thick grey blankets. Khaled reached out and pulled the blanket aside.

A cry escaped from Maya. Pam's blonde hair shimmered against the pillow, her eyes were closed, her face pale as death.

'Mum!' Maya shouted, throwing herself down beside the still figure. But, though she wrapped her arms around her and kissed her, Pam didn't stir. 'Wake up!' Maya shrilled, shaking her. There was no response.

'What have they done to her?' she yelled at Khaled.

'She's drugged. She'll come out of it. Don't worry. She'll be all right.'

As he spoke, Pam's eyelids flickered and for a brief moment Maya saw the soft grey of her eyes, but then they shut tight again. Maya stroked her face and kissed her. Pam's eyes opened again but didn't focus; she gazed at Maya with a glassy stare.

'What have they given her?'

'Just something to keep her quiet. It'll wear off.

She tried to escape.'

Maya looked at her mum's bloodless face. 'She needs help,' she said.

Getting up, she rushed at the door with a flying kick, then banged on it with her fists and shouted, 'Help! Help! My mum needs help.'

Khaled grabbed her, pinning her arms to her sides. 'Don't,' he warned. 'Don't make trouble or he'll kill us all. He's got nothing to lose.'

From somewhere above them came a loud bang.

'What the hell was that?' Maya asked. 'Are they raiding the place? I wanted a few MI5 agents, not the whole bloody army.'

'I sent Simon your message,' Khaled said. 'This isn't his doing. Maybe it's been taken out of his hands.'

She stared at him. 'One helicopter that's all I wanted.'

Khaled loosened his grip on her arm, his handsome face set into grim lines. 'He'll send it, he won't let you down.'

'Whatever happens, we have to save Omar,' Maya said. 'He's the only one who can give orders to stop the bombing.'

She went over to her mum and stroked her hair;

she was sleeping soundly. Khaled came and stood beside her.

Another loud bang came from outside. They looked at one another, their eyes softening. 'I'm frightened,' Maya whispered.

Khaled put a hand on her shoulder. 'I have prayed. We won't fail.'

'I have to go,' she said. 'I have to get to Omar.'

Khaled stiffened. 'No, it's too dangerous.'

Maya almost smiled. 'It's all been dangerous.' Going over to Pam, she bent down and hugged her.

'Love you, Mum.'

Pam's eyes flickered.

'Don't worry,' Maya told her. 'I'll get you out of here.'

Pushing a pillow under her head to make her more comfortable, Maya turned to Khaled. 'Right,' she said. 'Did you unlock the vent?'

He nodded.

'How many men does Omar have?'

'About fifteen.'

'Help me up to the window.'

'No,' he protested. 'Let me go instead.'

Maya shook her head. 'They'll shoot you.' She pushed him out of the way and went over to the window. 'Look after Pam.'

Khaled stood on a chair and tried to open the small oblong window, but it wouldn't budge. Maya grabbed a piece of old piping, climbed on the chair and smashed at the window. It was safety glass and hardly cracked.

'Stand back,' Khaled said. He snatched the pipe and slammed it into the pane. After a few attempts the glass smashed into fine cobwebs.

'OK. Let me stand on your shoulders,' Maya ordered.

From her precarious position she took the piping and smashed out jagged shards from the frame. Then she levered herself up and put her head through the window. Immediately a burst of fire zipped across the yard, ricocheting off the stone walls. Khaled dragged her back inside and they collapsed onto the floor.

'You can't do it, they've spotted you.'

'No, it was just coincidence. They were firing above me.'

She caught up a sheet, tore off a strip and tied it to the piping.

'Insurance,' she said. 'Heave me up.'

Climbing on Khaled's shoulders again she put

her head through the window. This time there was no response. 'Give me the pipe.'

It was a tight squeeze. Her jacket tore and a piece of glass pierced her arm, but with Khaled's help she managed to wriggle through the small window which gave onto the yard outside at ground level.

Before her the yard glowed white in a blaze of floodlights; over the boundary wall she saw silhouettes of armoured vehicles. It was dangerous to move, and yet she had to risk it. Slowly, slowly, she edged towards the back of the building.

* * *

Omar and his men were cocooned in an upstairs room.

'We're surrounded,' Nazim said. 'What do we do?'

The men looked at Omar. He was loading a pistol. 'We fight,' he said.

'There are massive weapons out there,' Nazim said.

'They won't fire on us,' Omar said. 'They know the girl and her mother are in here. And they want us alive.'

'They might want you, but they don't care a damn about us,' Nazim snapped back.

Omar's lip curled. 'You'll die as martyrs,' he said.

Nazim stared at him. 'I'm not giving up without a fight. We've fixed two machine guns, there are some grenades downstairs. Who's with me?'

Several of the men shouted their support, then they ran down the stairs into the bottom loading bay, leaving Omar to his fate.

Chapter Twenty-four

Maya slid along the wall under the shadow of the roof until she reached the corner, then crept silently round the back of the mill. It was totally dark there. Her hands clawed at the gritty stone, feeling for the vent. At last she touched flat, smooth metal. Her fingers found the handle, she pulled hard.

At first it wouldn't budge, it was too heavy. She gritted her teeth as she bent and pulled with all her might. Her injured hand was weak. She was beginning to think she'd have to go back for Khaled, when she gave one last mighty tug and the cover moved. She pulled again and managed to get her arm inside to lever it open. Pushing with her shoulder, she eased her body inside.

It was tight. She jammed her arms against the

sides, pulled up her knees and edged forward. Slowly she slid along the tunnel. Blackness surrounded her. It seemed to take forever to reach the end but, just as Khaled had foretold, her hand eventually touched the rung of a steel ladder. Her fingers traced the bottom rung.

Raising her arm over her head, she felt the space above, then her hands found the higher rungs, her feet got a purchase and she pulled herself up. Still holding onto the piece of piping she climbed, hand over hand.

The rungs were slippery, her feet faltered, but she hung on, up and up until her head touched something solid. *Bump!* Not a heavy knockout blow but a gentle bang. She'd reached the manhole cover. If Khaled had loosened it, then she should be able to push herself up and through.

She hoisted herself onto the top step and pushed with her head; the cover wobbled. With a mighty effort she moved it to one side, then placing her elbows on either side of the hole, she levered herself up.

A single beam from the floodlights sliced the room, lighting up old machinery and wooden posts. She was on the first floor, the grinding room of the mill; she'd memorised the layout of the building as Khaled had described it and, swift as water, she ran to hide in a dark corner near the stairs. Heart pounding, she waited and listened. There was an ominous silence outside and in the building everything was quiet. Then, through the tall mill windows, she saw a blue light arcing from the sky and heard the welcome throb of a helicopter. She was close, so close.

Leaving the dark corner, she darted towards a door at the end of the room. A siren split the night sky. She sensed their presence – masked armed men, black flak jackets, canisters of tear gas, guns at the ready.

Wait, please wait, she prayed.

Carefully opening the heavy fire door, she slid through and, just as Khaled had said, she was in a stone corridor. Go to the left, no – the right, the right passage led to Omar's headquarters. She edged towards the door, ears straining for the slightest sound, legs trembling. Looking through a small, square glass window, she saw Omar. He was sitting at a table with his back to her.

One quick step and she wrenched open the door. Before he had time to turn round, she darted forward and jabbed the pipe into his neck.

'Don't move, or I'll shoot.'

His hand flew backwards to grasp at what he thought was a gun, but Maya slammed the pipe into his ear. He yelped, reeling with pain, blindly groping for his own gun in front of him on the table. Maya beat him to it, snatching up the pistol, she pointed it at his forehead. His eyes bulged, a low groaning sound came from his open mouth.

'Shut up! Don't make a sound,' she told him. 'Now walk.'

Praying that his men wouldn't come charging back upstairs, Maya moved him along the corridor and up to the loft. At one end was a stone platform where sacks of corn had once been hoisted up for milling. Wooden shutters closed it off from the sky.

'Open the shutters,' she commanded.

Omar's breathing was unsteady, his hands were shaking.

'No,' he said.

'If you don't do it, I'll shoot you,' she snapped.

'What's the difference?' he moaned. 'You're going to push me off, anyway.'

'I'm not going to push you off. Listen!'

The sound of a helicopter throbbed above them.

'I'm going to rescue you.'

She clicked back the safety catch of the gun. 'Open the doors.'

When he bent to draw back the bolts, a blast of wind rushed in; the helicopter was hovering overhead.

'Get out there with your hands up,' Maya ordered.

He was whimpering as he stepped out onto the platform. From behind him, Maya waved the piping with the shred of white sheet still attached to one end.

Soft thuds sounded on the roof. Maya started forward, but mistaking her movement for an attack, Omar yelled. 'No!'

He turned and, with surprising agility, leapt forward and head-butted her. *Smash!* Maya's head snapped back, she crashed into a wooden beam and for a split second saw stars. As she reeled blindly, it was easy for Omar to grab her arms and grapple her to the edge of the platform. Her foot slipped over the edge, she toppled sideways, grabbed at a metal pole and just managed to save herself from plunging to her death.

Desperately she clung to the pole as Omar's face loomed close. His bony hand closed over hers;

she smelt the sourness of his breath as he tried to prise her fingers open. She spat in his face. He reared back in distaste. Swinging in mid-air, her feet scrabbled madly for a foothold. Her arms were on fire – any second she'd plummet to the ground. Hope was almost gone, she couldn't hold on any longer. Omar was coming for her again; her hands started to slip.

Shadows danced past her, black shapes flew through the air. As if by magic, Omar was lifted up and flew backwards. Strong hands grabbed Maya's arms and held her, a harness was slipped under her armpits and clipped round her chest. She was hauled up onto the platform and, like a lifeless dummy, she fell into somebody's arms.

It took her a moment to recover, then she raised her head and saw the sweep of Simon's blond hair.

'What took you so long?' she asked.

* * *

Omar looked a sad figure. His smart, shiny suit was spattered with dirt, his thick hair had blown into a quiff, his tie dangled from his shoulder. In this state he was handcuffed and dumped on the floor like a sack of potatoes.

'How many men are down there?' Simon asked him.

Omar didn't answer. Simon put a gun to his head.

'A few, maybe five or six,' Omar wheezed.

'About fifteen,' Maya told Simon. 'And they're armed. But we've disabled the submachine guns.'

Agents in black flak jackets and balaclavas swung onto the platform and dashed into the loft.

'My mum and Khaled are down there,' Maya said urgently to Simon. 'I don't want them to get hurt.'

'Where are they?'

'In the basement. I'll show you.'

'No, it's too dangerous. Stay up here.'

Maya ran to the top to the stairs. 'You can't stop me,' she said, 'not now.'

Simon pulled her back. 'All right. Stay behind me and keep your head down.'

He started to move down the stairs behind his men. All was quiet until they'd nearly reached the floor below, when there was a spatter of automatic gunfire.

'You told me you'd taken the clips,'

Simon spluttered.

'I did.'

'They must have fixed some. We have to respond, we have no choice.'

He gave his men the order to return fire, pushed Maya's head down and, crouching in front of her, provided a human shield. Another burst of fire came from below – one of the men in front groaned and fell.

'Stay back,' Simon ordered. But Maya moved forward as the men advanced down the stairs, squeezing past the injured man.

Another burst of gunfire came from below. Bullets zinged past, hitting the ceiling. Maya covered her ears, her hands were shaking. Chunks of plaster fell, dust filled her mouth. Coughing and choking, she crawled forwards. They reached the first floor.

'We'll rush the basement,' Simon said in hushed tones. 'Wait for the signal.'

'Please be careful, Mum's down there,' Maya whispered.

Simon edged his way to the top step, then punched the air – his men scrambled downwards. There was an unearthly scream followed by a shattering explosion. Smoke rose.

'Oh my God! Mum!'

Leaping down the steps, Maya reached the bottom, then dodged back and hid in the space underneath them. Smoke filled her mouth, she tied her headscarf over her face and crawled forwards along the corridor. Her knees scraped on the stone floor, her head was screaming with noise as Simon's team fired round after round towards Omar's men.

Staying just behind Simon's men, she reached the door of the room where Pam was imprisoned. It took all her courage to stand up.

The door was locked. She rammed her shoulder against it, but it wouldn't give. As she tried again, a round of bullets slammed into a wall close by; dust and debris stung her cheeks. Desperate for help, she looked back and saw a robed figure coming towards her. Instantly she recognized the wide face and huge eyes shining beneath the hijab.

'Lubna, help me, please. My mum and Khaled are in there.'

Lubna nodded and held out a key. 'Here,' she said. 'I'll open the door.'

Ignoring the gunfire, she calmly unlocked the door and went inside. Maya shot in after her. Pam was still lying on the bed but there was no sign of

Khaled – he must have escaped through the window.

Maya gestured towards her mum. 'Help me get her out of here.'

Lubna shook her head. 'I can't.' Then she smiled, and putting her hand inside the neck of her jacket, she pulled out an amulet. 'We will die in glory,' she said. Her gaze was unflinching, her eyes glowing with fervour. 'I will be in paradise.'

Maya's heart flipped, her insides turned to mush. She understood what Lubna intended to do. The amulet was a detonator.

Taking a step backwards, Maya tried to reason with her. 'Lubna, don't, please, don—' she breathed. But before her sentence was finished, Khaled ran into the room, then stopped dead as he took stock of what was happening.

'Lubna,' he said, gently. 'Lubna, the time is not yet come.'

He stepped towards her, reaching out to touch her arm.

She pulled back. 'Traitor,' she spat at him. 'You have betrayed our cause.'

Her eyes flashed fire, and at that moment Maya knew they were doomed. Khaled knew it too. Just as Lubna's hand moved to grip the detonator, he grabbed her and pitched her back against the far wall.

A mighty echoing boom filled Maya's ears. She was thrown to the floor, all the air sucked out of her. Dazzling lights flowered in her head, she span in a dark, soundless tunnel and carried on spinning – lost to the world while battle raged.

Lying in a silent cocoon, her brain shut down. She had no awareness of the wind blowing in through a giant hole in the wall, or of her mother slowly rolling from her bed and crawling towards her. Gentle hands touched her face. Pam bent close, her grimy cheeks streaked with tears. Coughing into the dusty air, she marshalled all her strength to cradle her daughter in her arms, lifting Maya's head and whispering her name over and over again.

Maya opened her eyes. It was impossible to speak, her throat was cracked and dry and no sound would come out. Her legs were shaking uncontrollably but she had to get up, she had to see.

Leaning against each other for support, mother and daughter limped over to the far corner of the room where two bodies lay. They were lifeless, unmoving. Lubna's headscarf was no longer white, but stained red; one of her arms had been blown off; jagged shards of bone lay in a pool of blood; at the end of the severed arm, the fingers were clenched round the amulet.

Khaled was lying on his back. His head at an odd angle, an arm flung out. There was a smear of blood on the side of his face and more blood pumping from a hole in his leg; his eyes were closed.

Maya bent down and put her head to his chest. His heart was beating.

'We've got to get help,' Maya rasped, her eyes pricking with tears.

Pam's lips moved but Maya couldn't hear the reply because her ears were still ringing from the blast. She pointed to her ears to make Pam understand. Pam nodded, glanced down at Khaled, back at Maya, then she started to pull sheets off the bed. Maya helped her tear them into strips and Pam wadded the sheeting and pressed it against Khaled's leg to stop the flow of blood. Khaled moaned, as Pam bound the leg and tied off the thick bandage. She put her hand on his wrist.

'He's OK,' she mouthed. 'His pulse is strong.'

For the first time, Maya noticed how grey her mum's face looked, and then she realised her own hands and clothes were covered in thick dust and spattered with blood. There were holes in her T-shirt. She lifted it up and saw blood oozing from a deep cut just above her waist.

Pressing a piece of sheeting to the cut, she watched her mum wipe Khaled's face and gently pull pieces of rubble from his hair. There was nothing they could do for Lubna. Her face was turned towards them, the plump cheeks spotted with moles were unmarked, her lips frozen in a half-smile and the big brown eyes that had shone with laughter almost closed. If you only saw her face, it would be easy to think she was sleeping, but the hijab, the sign of her faith, was soaked with blood.

When the flow of blood from her own wound had eased, Maya knelt down and took Khaled's hand. He didn't stir, but she was sure he squeezed her fingers.

Her mum leant towards her, gripping her arm and motioning towards the door. She was saying something, but Maya's ears were still buzzing and she wasn't sure what her mum was trying to tell her; they couldn't escape while the firing was still going on.

She shook her head, sniffed and swallowed. Her

ears popped and her mum's words came through: 'It's stopped, thank God, it's stopped.'

And Maya realised that the firing *had* stopped. In the wondrous silence they fell on each other, hugging for all they were worth.

One of the Simon's team appeared in the doorway. 'Omar's men have surrendered, the paramedics are on their way.'

'Come on, my brave girl,' Pam said. 'We're going home.'

* * *

The medics had been on stand-by, and in a few moments they were climbing over the debris with stretchers. A doctor arrived and took charge. She could do nothing for Lubna, but set up a drip into Khaled's arm, gave him injections and supervised his journey to the waiting ambulance.

Maya insisted on walking to the ambulance. Her head was throbbing, her legs shaky and she was bleeding, but she didn't want to be stretchered out. Holding Pam's hand, she walked into the mill yard just in time to see Omar being taken away. Surrounded by men from Simon's team who were leading him into a secure military-type vehicle, he was handcuffed. A stooped, shambling figure – he looked pathetic.

Pam shook her head. 'Incredible that one little man had so much power.'

'He hasn't now,' Maya said. 'He's finished.'

Pam put her arm round her daughter. 'I can't believe what you did,' she said.

Maya shook her head. 'Neither can I.'

'You were amazing,' her mum said proudly.

'I did have some help at the end,' she said. 'Khaled and Simon came through for me.'

'But it was your plan. Khaled told me. He said it was your idea to capture Omar's father.'

Maya nodded. Suddenly she felt very proud. 'I had to act quickly, or Omar would have killed you. I didn't give up, even when I thought Khaled had betrayed me.'

'He had to make them believe he was on their side – right till the end.'

'Yeah, I know, I just hope he'll be all right.'

The ambulance carrying Khaled sped away. They stayed and watched Omar being driven away and then walked to the waiting ambulance. As the doors closed, Maya looked back at the mill.

'Poor Lubna,' she said. 'She had so much to live for.'

'And so much to die for,' Pam added.

Maya gave her mum a puzzled look. 'I don't think anything is worth dying for,' she said.

'Are you sure about that?' Pam asked, hugging her daughter.

Chapter Twenty-five

Four weeks later on a Sunday afternoon, a taxi drew up outside the Begum Emporium fruit shop, and a tall dark girl and a small blonde woman got out clutching flowers, bags and parcels. They paid the driver and as they walked towards the shop, the girl pointed to a café across the road.

'I was sitting over there when I saw Omar's men going into Mariam's,' she said. 'I was so scared when I saw Nazim. I knew he was out for revenge.'

'And now he's dead,' Pam said. 'Killed in the fighting at the mill.'

'Yep, his brother was on TV – boasting that Nazim is a martyr.'

'I saw it,' Pam said bitterly. 'Unfortunately it was exactly the sort of publicity he wanted.'

She held the flowers aloft like a symbol of peace. 'Here, you take these. Let's enjoy our visit.'

They rang the bell at the side of the shop door. There was a flurry of activity inside, the bolts were drawn back and Mariam stood in the doorway, her smile as wide as the door.

'Welcome. I'm so happy to see you. And Maya, all in one piece after your battle.' She reached out and took Maya's hands in hers, kissing them eagerly. 'Khaled told me how brave you were.'

Glowing with pride, Maya gave her the flowers and Mariam buried her face in the creamy white petals.

'They're beautiful, thank you,' she said.

'This is my mum, Pam,' Maya told her.

Pam stepped forward and put a hand on Mariam's arm. 'Thank you for helping Maya,' she said. 'It must have been frightening for you, defying Omar and his men.'

Mariam lowered her head. 'It was my duty,' she said. 'Please come, come on in.'

They followed her up the stairs into the bright sitting room.

Khaled was lying on the sofa, but when he saw them, he swung his legs down and hoisted himself to his feet.

'No, no, sit down,' Maya said, rushing forwards. 'You should rest.'

He laughed. 'I've done enough resting in hospital.' He reached for a crutch that was leaning against the sofa and, quickly placing it under his armpit, he straightened up. 'There, see!' He found his balance and raised the crutch in the air. 'I'm healed!'

'Not quite yet,' Mariam said.

Pam came forward and looked him up and down, shaking her head. 'Khaled, it's so good to see you. How are you?'

'I'm fine. Every day it's a little better.'

'His leg was badly damaged,' Mariam said, 'but the doctors say that with lots of physiotherapy and exercise, he should be able to walk well again.'

'And I'm being a good boy and doing all the exercises. Look!'

Tentatively he slid one leg forward, got his balance and moved the other leg to meet it. It took ages for him to take another step, and the look of absolute concentration on his face made Maya's heart turn over. When he reached the armchair, he put out his hands to take his weight and collapsed.

Maya went over to him. 'Hey, you're doing really

well.' Looking down at him, she saw tiny beads of sweat sparkling on his forehead. 'Is it still painful?'

'Only when I dance,' he said wryly.

Pam came over to join them. 'You saved our lives,' she said to Khaled.

'I'm not sure about that,' he replied. 'Maya did most of the work.'

'But if you hadn't acted so quickly, we'd all be dead. Thank you is not enough for what you did, but,' she reached out her hand, 'thank you.'

Khaled shook her hand and smiled, but the smile was tinged with sadness. 'Poor Lubna,' he said. 'If only Omar hadn't got to her, she'd be here too. All that education, and yet she believed him.'

'So sad for her and her family,' Pam said.

'They're shattered,' Khaled told them. 'They knew nothing about her involvement with the Brotherhood.'

'It's hard to figure out,' Maya said. 'She helped me escape, then wanted to kill me.'

Mariam set a tray of drinks and snacks down on the coffee table. 'Lubna, like so many of our young people, was confused and misled,' she said. 'Torn between two cultures: they think the West is sinful and materialistic, they condemn it and yet they're tempted by it. The burden of that dichotomy is heavy.'

Khaled rested one hand on his aunt's shoulder.

'It's true,' he said. 'They despise their parents for bringing them to such a heathen country and look back to their homeland, searching for answers. Islamism offers them a simple path, one way – the way of jihad.'

'Lubna was brainwashed,' Pam said.

'I suppose that for her, it was the right thing to do,' Maya said.

'She could have killed us all,' Pam said quietly.

A heavy silence hung in the air, then Khaled turned to Maya. 'Thank you for the card and books. They were very welcome.'

'Did you get my letter?' she asked.

'Yes, I did. Brilliant cartoon of you driving the furniture van.'

'And the crash. Did you see how I'd drawn us hiding on the building site while all the police vans arrived?'

'You never told me about that,' Pam said.

'Er, no,' Maya said quickly. 'Forget I said that.'

Khaled looked at Pam. 'So what about Omar?'

'He's given us all the information we need.

Squealed like a rat – names, addresses. We've put most of his followers out of action and have plenty of evidence to put them away for a long time. For the moment, the UK and the rest of Europe is a safer place.'

'But for how long?' Khaled asked.

Pam raised her eyebrows. 'I'm realistic,' she said. 'Until all borders are undisputed, until all people are free – there'll be terrorism. Plus, some people look for any excuse to commit atrocities.'

'Yeah, some like Omar – on a power trip,' Khaled added.

Pam nodded her agreement, then gave him a brief smile. 'But I couldn't do my job if I didn't have hope.'

'It's Omar's family I feel sorry for,' Mariam said. 'His daughters are good girls and his father, Sharif, is a lovely, well-respected man.'

'I'd like to meet him,' Pam said. 'I didn't have a chance to talk to him at the mill.'

'Mum, you weren't in a fit state to talk to anybody,' Maya pointed out.

'I'm sure Sharif would like to talk to you,' Mariam said, as she poured drinks. 'It's troubled him greatly that Omar was planning such things.

He was here yesterday, inquiring after Khaled. He knows you're working to release Majid. It's so strange – two sons, such opposites.'

She straightened up and smiled at Pam. 'His granddaughter's looking after him. I think he'd like the opportunity to talk, to get things straight. I'll see if I can arrange it. Now, please sit down and have some of my home-made lemonade and snacks. My husband will be here soon, then we'll have dinner.' She backed away. 'If you'll just excuse me a moment, I have something cooking on the stove.'

'I'll help you,' Pam said. 'I'm sure these two have heaps to talk about.'

Left alone, there was a short awkward silence between Khaled and Maya. There was so much to say, and yet neither of them spoke. Khaled pressed the palms of his hands together, Maya sat opposite him on the sofa biting her fingernails. Khaled leaned forward and rubbed gently at his knee.

'Is it sore?'

He nodded. Their eyes met.

'Thanks,' Maya said. 'Thanks for helping me. I'm so sorry you got hurt.'

Khaled smiled, a smile that reached his eyes, crinkling the corners. 'It's OK,' he said. 'And you didn't give me much choice about helping. You were pretty scary.'

'Sorry about the gun.'

'I'm not sure which was worse, the gun or your driving.'

'I was scared stiff when you were going to hand me over to Omar. So I guess we're quits.'

There was a rattle of pans from the kitchen and Maya could hear Pam and Mariam talking. 'They're getting on well,' she said. 'I knew they would.'

'What about you?' Khaled said. 'Are you OK?'

Maya was thoughtful. 'Yeah, mostly. It helps to know Omar's locked up. I'm actually looking forward to getting back to school and normality. What will you do?'

Khaled's expression grew serious. 'I can't stay here. Special Branch is protecting me but I'll have to disappear soon, and while I'm here, I'm putting Mariam at risk. To some I'm a hero – to others, a traitor.'

'Where will you go?'

'I want to study.'

'Where?'

'I can't tell you.'

A shadow fell across Maya's face. Khaled leaned back against the armchair, his eyes taking in her disappointment. 'If Allah wills it, we'll meet again.'

'I hope so,' Maya said

Khaled glanced round, as if somebody might be listening. 'You go to school in London, don't you?

'Yes.'

'There are many universities in London.'

'One's right next to my school,' Maya said.

Khaled nodded. 'One day, a penniless student might appear.'

'A penniless, limping student?'

'A penniless, limping student in disguise,' Khaled laughed.

'You promise?

'I promise.'

'Will you carry on working for the Intelligence Service?'

'I think so, when they need me. It's important work.'

'You must be careful.'

Khaled smiled. 'I'm always careful. There was only a problem when a certain beautiful young woman stepped into my bookshop.'

'Sorry,' Maya said with mock solemnity.

'You were looking for enlightenment. Did you find it?'

Maya's forehead puckered as she gave his question some thought. 'Not really, but I have changed. My family – my Muslim family who died in Kosovo – I didn't want to know about them, I wouldn't let myself remember – it was too painful. Pam used to try and get me to connect with them . . . you know . . . she gave me books about Islam, tried to get me interested, but I thought. . . I can't say it, it's difficult.'

She paused, looking down, then raised her eyes and looked at him. 'I was angry . . . I sort of thought they were stupid to die for their religion, but now I see it wasn't their choice. They were killed just for being who they were, just for being in the wrong place.'

Khaled nodded.

'That night here, when Uncle Ali prayed,' Maya continued, 'I remembered, I think I remembered my father's voice – it was sort of comforting, familiar.'

'So, would you like to learn more?'

'About being Muslim?'

'About your family and Islam."

287

Maya screwed her face up in thought. 'I'm not sure about the religious stuff. The thing is, if you totally submit to something, you stop asking questions.'

Khaled nodded. 'That can be a problem,' he said. 'But it doesn't have to be like that.'

'And I couldn't buy into some of the rules and the treatment of women.'

'It's not Islam that's at fault, it's the way people interpret it,' Khaled said. 'I don't think we're so very different. Most Muslims want a good job, a happy family life and the chance to do some good.'

Maya leaned forward and eyed him sternly. 'So, why did you get involved with Omar and all that militant stuff?'

'It wasn't militant at first. We produced leaflets setting out our true beliefs, informing people. The Western press is biased – look at the way they report any news about the Middle East. If a British soldier is killed in Iraq, it's front page news, if two hundred Iraqis die in a bomb blast, it's on the back page. Our voices aren't heard. I wanted to do something positive. At first the bookshop was just a small centre which held meetings, discussion groups, but when Omar took over, it got out of hand. And then I had to stop him, I had no choice.'

Maya watched the memories dance across his face; her eyes lingered on his, gazing into the shimmering green irises, deep and mysterious.

'I have something for you,' he said, reaching into his pocket. 'Close your eyes.'

Maya did as she was told and Khaled took her hand, turned it over and placed something in her palm. When she opened her eyes she saw her ring, the ruby glittering like fire.

'How did you. . .?'

'Don't ask. Just be happy.'

Leaning back, he reached for something that was on the table behind him. 'I have something else.'

He handed Maya a roll of thick parchment tied with purple ribbon. After carefully untying the ribbon, she unrolled the paper and saw beautifully executed Arabic characters precisely drawn in black ink.

'It's beautiful,' she said. 'What does it say?'

'It's from Khalil Gibran's *The Prophet*. I copied it when I was in hospital.'

'Can you translate it?'

He nodded.

'*And if our hands should meet in another dream, we shall build another tower in the sky.*'

Maya tasted the words, rolled them round on her

tongue, asked him to repeat them.

'I like that,' she said. 'To dream, to hope – to make the world a better place. I think that's what we tried to do.'

Read more about Maya Brown and her adventures at
http://www.mayabrownmissions.co.uk.

Read on for an exclusive preview
of the first chapter of
Maya's next adventure in

Breaking the Circle

Chapter One

The girl stood stone still in the middle of the pavement. She was small and thin, dressed in black – scuffed leather jacket, tight, frayed jeans and worn boots. Her clothes were too heavy, her face too pale for such a hot late summer day. Beneath a strand of lank, gold hair her eyes moved restlessly, scanning the people hurrying home.

As Maya drew closer, she was aware that the girl was watching her. When she was level, the girl stepped into her path.

'Got any spare change?'

Maya stopped, patted her pockets, gave an apologetic shrug and shook her head. She couldn't give money to everybody. This area was getting worse, full of crazy people living on the edge.

The girl repeated her request, her voice sharper, more insistent.

A sour smell of sweat came off her as she raised a cupped hand in front of Maya's face. Irritated, Maya reeled back, ready to walk away, but the girl whispered something – words in a foreign language, words that were strange yet also familiar. Words which were no doubt curses, but they sent Maya's thoughts spinning. She looked into the girl's face; the eyes that stared back were a startling, luminous gold. Maya felt as though she'd been zapped.

Despite the heat, a shiver ran through her. She tore her eyes away from the girl and stumbled forward. As she walked away, she felt the girl's eyes burning into her skin.

A few steps ahead, Maya knew the girl was following; she could hear her leather jacket rustling, her black boots scuffing the pavement. A split-second decision – should she take the short cut? Her heartbeat quickened as she turned into the narrow alleyway – she wouldn't be bullied into going the long way round.

Keeping her steps deliberate and measured, she walked along the hard dirt path between high walls, a skinny girl at her back – a girl who looked unwashed and in need of a good meal. No worries, she could sort her out if she had to.

The alley was littered with broken glass, plastic bags and weeds. As Maya dodged the debris, the girl's boots scraped behind her, kicking at a bottle and sending it spinning. A thin tabby cat sprang from the shadows and clawed up the side of the wall. Moving to the edge of the path, Maya stopped and switched her heavy bag to the other shoulder, alert, listening – the girl had stopped too.

Up ahead, the sun was still shining, silhouetting blocks of tall flats against blue sky – beyond them, the park and home. With determined steps, Maya strode forward. If she hadn't stayed at school for athletics practice she'd be home by now, finishing schoolwork, looking forward to watching *Hollyoaks*. She had no regrets about the races, though – she'd thrashed everybody. A thrill of pride ran through her as she remembered the last race; five hundred metres and she'd clocked a personal best. Soon it would be the inter-schools championship. Bring it on! She was ready.

Head down, plotting a race strategy, she forgot

about the girl following. She didn't see the guy behind a screen of bushes, was totally unaware of the girl taking out a mobile and speaking into it softly, urgently. The first thing she knew was a swish of movement at her heels, a tug at her blazer, a bony hand clamping her shoulder.

'Give me money. Give me mobile.' The girl's eyes were like a cat's, liquid amber glowing in her face. 'You, you give me.'

'No!'

Slow to react to a sharp push, Maya was sent reeling. She hit the ground – *whack!*

Fight back, fight back!

Fingers clutched her hair, twisting and wrenching; her schoolbag was ripped from her shoulder.

Charged with anger, Maya swung into action, lashing out, lunging for her bag, grasping the strap. The girl tugged hard but Maya's training kicked in. Reeling the girl in like a fish, she held her tight, then relaxed her grip for a vital split-second. Sensing victory, the girl pulled back, but at that precise moment Maya yanked her down, put an armlock round her neck and rolled her onto her stomach.

'You can't have my bag, right?' Maya said, pushing the girl's head down.

The girl mumbled, her mouth full of dirt.

'Who are you?' Maya asked, jolting the girl's head.

'Get off. Let go!' the girl spluttered, kicking wildly.

Maya held her down. Then a man's voice shouted, 'Leave 'er!'

Hoping for help, Maya glanced over her shoulder. She gulped. A snarling dog was charging towards her, ears pricked, eyes like laser pens, its slavering jaws bared in a vicious snarl. Her eyes were riveted, muscles tensed, but she couldn't move – there was nowhere to run. The dog was so close that any moment now it would sink its teeth into her skin. At a command from the man, the dog dropped into the dirt. A low, savage growl came from its throat, clumps of froth fell from its mouth.

'What's up? Scared?'

A young guy in a black hoodie ambled towards her, his face sharp and bony, eyes half-hidden by the shadow of the hood. As he bent to clip the dog onto a silver chain, she noticed his long, thin nose; his lips turned up in a mocking smile.

A snappy response to his stupid question went through Maya's head.

Too right I'm scared. Isn't that the reason you have that rabid dog with you – to scare the guts out of people?

But she couldn't speak. The dog was hypnotising her with its mad stare, and all the time it was snarling and slavering as if contemplating its next meal. Fear sang through her bones.

They can smell you, they can smell fear.

The boy sniffed and spat as Maya slowly, very slowly, eased herself off the girl, who was still underneath her, and rolled away from the dog.

'Gimme the bag,' the boy ordered.

Maya hesitated – there was no way she was putting her arm near that crazy dog.

'Give it 'ere.'

He yanked the dog away from her as he reached out his hand. The dog pulled sideways sending the guy slightly off-balance. Fast as lightning, Maya dipped a hand into the bag and grabbed her mobile. It was just going into her pocket when he spotted it.

'I'll have that,' he said. 'Get it, Kay.'

The girl, who'd been silent and still ever since he appeared, levered herself up, limped over and went to take the mobile but Maya clutched it to her chest.

'It's mine. You can't take it!'

The girl backed away, looking puzzled and uncertain. She tugged at the zip of her leather jacket, hunched her shoulders and stared down at the ground, biting her knuckles. The fight had gone out of her, but the boy was on a mission and he took charge.

'I can have what I like, or Gunner'll have you. You don't wanna mess with Gunner.'

On cue, the dog snarled. Defeated, Maya opened her hand.

'Take it, Kay,' the boy said, laughing cruelly as the girl limped over and took the mobile. 'What you done to yourself?' he snapped.

The girl, Kay, winced as she put weight on her foot. 'My ankle is hurt.'

'Serves you right. What you doin', robbin' schoolgirls?'

'Is your fault, you ask me for money.'

'So, what you messin' at 'ere? Get back to base an' earn some proper cash.'

Kay sniffed. 'No. I not do that. I am your girl.'

He leaned forward. 'You're too particular. Think you're special?' He laughed. 'Come on, give that 'ere,' he added, indicating the mobile.

'No, is mine, is good. I sell it, give you money.'

A fist slammed into the girl's arm, sending the

phone flying. Maya saw her chance and didn't hesitate. She caught the mobile, veered round them and ran for her life. In a flash she saw the wall was slightly lower towards the end of the path and threw herself at it, leaping up, fingers clawing at the top of the wall as the dog came roaring towards her. Barking and yelping, it snapped at her heels. She kicked out, her foot connected, thudding into the dog's jaw, sending it reeling.

In the split-second it took the dog to recover, she managed to get one elbow on top of the wall. She was just swinging her legs up out of danger when the dog leapt wildly below her, catching a piece of her skirt in its teeth. It hung suspended by the cloth, a bite away from her flesh. She had to do something or it would mangle her leg. Jerking her body sideways, she smashed a fist down on Gunner's forehead. With a strangled gasp, the dog fell.

Triumphant, she hoisted herself up on top of the wall but her mobile slipped out of her hand. No time to retrieve it; the dog wasn't down and out. It was yelping and snapping again.

Time to jump!

Landing amongst big tufts of spiky grass, she scrambled to her feet and lurched forwards. There was nothing to use as a weapon – no stick or anything – but, over in the far corner, she spotted an old brick outbuilding. Racing towards it, she slipped on a sheet of glass. It shattered and a shard of glass razored her foot, but the pain only urged her onward. Behind her, she could hear the dog barking itself into a frenzy, scrabbling over the wall. In the nick of time she threw herself against the door of the building; mercifully it gave way, catapulting her into the sanctuary of the shed. She turned and kicked the door shut as the dog's nose appeared round the edge. Then, with trembling hands, she picked up a brick from a pile near the door and hammered home a rusty bolt.

Loud commands boomed over the wall. 'Gunner. Here, Gunner!'

Leaning against the door, she listened hard. On the other side the dog was panting; hot breath seeping through gaps in the door. Would the boy come after it?

Another command. 'Gunner, here! Come here, you useless piece of meat.'

The panting stopped. The grass rustled, broken glass crashed; there was a loud yelp. She waited, every nerve trembling, but the boy didn't come.

Standing in the empty building, she cursed the

girl who'd followed her, the scumbag in the hood, the mad dog and her own stupidity. Torn skirt, bleeding foot, scratched legs, nerves in shreds – why had she been so stubborn and taken the short cut? What an idiot! She should have trusted her instincts – she knew that girl was trouble as soon as she'd laid eyes on her.

Another shout came from a distance.

'What the. . .?' There were more words, the translation lost in the air. What felt like a lifetime passed. Several times she nearly pulled back the bolt on the door, but the thought of the boy and his killer dog lying in wait kept her inside. Pressing her ear to the wooden planks of the door, she heard the shout of children in the playground, and the distant drone of traffic. She turned her head and peered through a crack – nobody was visible, there was no sign of the dog, the guy, or the girl. Finally she screwed up her courage and ventured out, easing the door open bit by bit until she was sure there was no one waiting to ambush her.

Squinting into the evening sunlight, she scouted for an escape route. The waste ground was enclosed by high walls – the way she'd entered seemed the best way out. Carefully avoiding shards of glass and stopping to look and listen every few steps, she picked her way over to the wall. The ground was lower on this side, the wall high, but a few flying attempts to get a foothold paid off and she was able to swing her legs up and over and drop down onto the path.

A nervous glance up and down the track confirmed that there was no sign of the hooded thug or his dog. So, top priority was to search for her mobile, but she knew right away it had gone. Of course, the boy had spotted it and picked it up. He'd taken her schoolbag containing books and money, her purse containing her bank card, but most upsetting was the loss of the phone that Pam had given her just before she left. It was a secure number which Pam, her mum, might call at any moment. Now, she wouldn't be able to answer. A mixture of sadness and anger welled up as she looked again in the spot where she was certain she'd dropped it. It wasn't there. She kicked at a bottle and swore loudly.

Damn him for stealing her mobile! It was complicated enough to stay in touch with her mum without added problems.

Nothing for it but to head home. She walked warily towards the playground at the end of the path. Children were playing on swings, a couple of men were walking dogs. It was a lovely summer's evening.

Gran would be waiting for her in the flat, but she couldn't even call to tell her she'd be late.

As she crossed in front of a playground on the edge of the estate, a couple of young boys ran up to her – shaved heads, cheeky grins.

'Give us fifty p!' the smallest one demanded.

'No, go away.'

'Go on, tight arse.'

'Shove off. I haven't got any money. Some thieving yob just nicked my purse.'

The boys started to laugh. 'That'd be Gerard. We just seen 'im.'

'He went that way wiv 'is dog. He's cool, Gerard.'

'Oh yeah. Very cool, with his mad dog and thieving girlfriend.'

'His girlfriend's over there.'

A stone whistled past Maya's ear as she walked towards the place the boys had pointed to. Skirting round some straggly bushes and two upturned shopping trolleys, she emerged into a concrete square and saw the girl, Kay, sitting on a low wall in front of a block of flats. She looked miserable, and made no effort to move as Maya walked up to her.

Agent profile
Name: S.M. HALL

Stated occupation: Teacher of English and Drama. (Has been spotted in classrooms in Qatar, Singapore, Malaysia and Bakewell.) Sometimes poses as a writer of fiction – *Circle of Fire* is the fifth novel.

Subversive activities: recently took part in a Bed-In for Peace in Liverpool; eats pistachios while typing.

Location: between Matlock Bath, Derbyshire and John Lennon's childhood home, 'Mendips' in Liverpool – a property owned by the National Trust. Is this a front for digging into matters of national security, such as John Lennon's alleged scrumping of apples from Strawberry Fields? Meets high-profile individuals who visit the house, but does not betray confidences.

Distinctive features: mole on right cheek, whorls on 8 fingertips, scalp double crowned. Eye colour changeable – grey, green or blue depending on mood. Small enough not to be noticed when following a suspect.

Known weapons: rolled-up newspaper, umbrella.

Potential liabilities: putting a foot in it; worrying; speaking French badly; shouting loudly at the TV when the England squad are playing football, "Pass, pass!"

Ambitions: to win the local pub quiz, to tell one funny joke, to grow six inches, hug a mountain gorilla, plant a tree in Nepal.

ALMOST TRUE
Keren David

Ruthless killers are hunting Ty. The police move him
and his mum to a quiet seaside town. But a horrific attack
and a bullet meant for Ty prove that he's not safe yet.

On the road again, Ty's in hiding with complete strangers . . .
who seem to know a lot about him. Meanwhile
he's desperate to see his girlfriend Claire, and terrified
that she may betray him. Ty can't trust his own judgement
and he's making dangerous decisions that could
deliver him straight to the gangsters.

A thrilling sequel to *When I Was Joe*,
shot through with drama and suspense.